THE DOUBLE

# THE DOUBLE

*A POEM OF ST. PETERSBURG*

F. M. DOSTOYEVSKY

*Translated by George Bird*

INDIANA UNIVERSITY PRESS

BLOOMINGTON & LONDON

SIXTH PRINTING 1971

COPYRIGHT © 1958 BY INDIANA UNIVERSITY PRESS

MANUFACTURED IN THE UNITED STATES OF AMERICA

LIBRARY OF CONGRESS CATALOG CARD NUMBER: 58-12204

253-20012-1   pa

# INTRODUCTION

With his second novel, *The Double*, Dostoyevsky made one of those brilliant experiments which characterize the brash young artist. His first novel, *Poor Folk*, had won him immediate acclaim, and he wanted to follow it with a display of sheer genius. But for critics and readers of that day, the experiment fizzled out; they found it tedious, thin and overlong, and even the author had to admit its faults: "I wrote a lot of it too quickly, and in moments of fatigue. The first half is better than the second. Alongside many brilliant passages are others so disgustingly bad that I can't read them myself." Some fifteen years later, however, he revised and improved the book for a collected edition of his work; and three years before his death, he could still write that he had never expressed a more serious idea in literature: it was the form of the tale which had "failed utterly."

As we know today, *The Double* contains the first open pronouncement of that "serious idea," the divided personality, which informs the whole of Dostoyevsky's achievement. Its technique is unresolved, but far from failing, it represents a bold advance beyond its sources, in Gogol and Hoffmann, toward the early tales of the modern symbolist, Franz Kafka. As an experiment, moreover, *The Double* almost works: its first half is a clever buildup toward psychological collapse; in the second half, which lags so badly, there are flashes of fine writing which move the story toward its strangely Kafkan climax. For the modern reader, trained on careful symbolism and hyper-refined analysis, *The Double* retains all the freshness of a pioneer effort, all the crude power, the unpretentious vigor, of a youthful stride toward psychological fiction.

Because of its modernity, *The Double* had baffled early readers. They could only compare it with Gogol's light satires on the vanities and desires of petty clerks. But Dostoyevsky's clerk, Mr. Golyadkin, is not a mere social type, like his models in "The Nose" and "The Diary of a Madman." He is instead the thin-skinned victim of social and bureaucratic pressures, and at the same time, his own executioner. Unable to cope with the anxieties of urban life, he responds either with defensive meekness and retirement, or with aggressive tactics which inevitably fail. It is significant that the double first appears after the clerk's eviction from a lavish party. When Golyadkin tries to attend this party, he is turned away at the door by servants. He creeps to the back stairs of the flat, however, and in a scene foreshadowing Kafka, he stands there in a dark corner, in the midst of rubbish and litter, gathering courage to enter. Finally he dashes into the midst of the ball and claims a dance with Klara Olsufyevna, the belle of the affair. Feeling strangely exhausted, he scrapes, stamps and stumbles when the dance begins. Klara utters a shriek, the crowd runs to her rescue, and Golyadkin is swept away by their forceful surge. After further confusion he is thrown out of the ball, and on his way home through the snow, he meets his double, his desire for aggressive social competence, released from within by the violent exclusion.

Here, in embryo, is the new idea which Dostoyevsky brought to Russian fiction: the combination of inward and outward pressures to produce a split in being which is somehow real. It was an idea which went beyond the simple good-and-evil equations behind other doubles of the age, like Poe's William Wilson or Dickens' Sidney Carton and Charles Darnay. In Dostoyevsky's own work, it led directly to a host of doubles and divided selves: to Raskolnikov's awareness, in *Crime and Punishment*, that Svidrigailov represents his own perverse desires; to Versilov's confession, in *A Raw Youth*, that a double stands beside him and prompts him to the most senseless actions; and finally, to Ivan Karamazov's vision of the devil as an actual presence, at the end of Dostoyevsky's career, when he was at last able to clarify the implicit premise of his early novel: namely, that dreams and hallucinations are real; that an unconscious self exists, opposing the conscious self; and that man is literally disunified in nature.

As scholars have long recognized, *The Double* provides a useful key to Dostoyevsky's growth in moral and intellectual power. It also points, in another direction, to his lesser-known role as formal innovator. In "The Nose," for instance, Gogol had spoofed the double theme in Hoffmann by dressing a nose in the costume of a state councillor, and sending its owner (a lowly clerk) in frantic search for it. He liked to parody Hoffmann, apparently, by placing his magical events in urban settings and exploiting their comic possibilities. But Dostoyevsky took this transfer seriously. He saw that Hoffmann's doubles *belonged* in the urban world which had produced them; that they were more at home, as it were, in flats and offices than in romantic settings. This alone was an advance over his models in aesthetic conception; but the problem of execution, of combining realism and fantasy, proved beyond his immediate powers. He seems to have worked here on three assumptions: first, that the double is produced by an acute state of hallucination in Golyadkin; second, that there is also an actual person, a new employee named Golyadkin, on whom the clerk projects his hallucination; and third, that the first two assumptions, properly handled, might create an illusion of the double's actuality, so as to suggest the reality of unconscious life. The first five chapters laid the groundwork for his realistic premise, the effect of hallucination; but in later chapters, when the effect of fantasy was introduced, the two premises began to compete for space and the writing became prolix and repetitious. George Bird, the translator of this edition, finds only praise for Dostoyevsky's technique, which certainly gains force and clarity from his deft translation. He fails to see, however, that a new idea calls for new means of expression, and that Dostoyevsky had merely improvised to meet this need.

The form which *The Double* called for was not hallucination, but a bold stroke of fantasy conveyed in realistic detail. It was not discovered until the fall of 1912, when the Czech genius, Franz Kafka, composed his first successful stories, "The Judgment" and *The Metamorphosis*. "The Judgment" owes little to Dostoyevsky, beyond the use of doubles, the business theme, the exchange of letters with an imaginary friend in Petersburg, and the horrendous verdict at the end, where a father condemns his son to death by drowning. In *The Metamorphosis*, however, the signs of Dostoyevsky's influence are extensive and detailed. One need only compare the opening paragraphs in each tale to catch them. As *The Double* opens, for instance, Golyadkin, a minor civil servant, awakens from a long night's rest "like a man as yet uncertain whether he is awake or still asleep, whether all at present going on about him is reality or a continuation of his disordered dreams." When he regains his senses, the walls of his little room look at him familiarly, and "the foul, murky, grey autumnal day" peers in at him through the window rather sourly. Golyadkin shuts his eyes again, "as though regretting his recently ended slumbers and wishing to recall them for a moment." Then he leaps from his bed, looks at himself in a mirror, and says: "A fine thing it would be if there was something wrong with me today . . . if something untoward had happened, and a strange pimple had come up, or something equally unpleasant." At the end of the day, five chapters later, the pimple does erupt in the form of a double, who plainly figures forth his illness.

In *The Metamorphosis*, Kafka telescopes this process, and

with a single stroke conveys the reality of unconscious life. For when Gregor Samsa, a commercial traveler, awakens one morning "from uneasy dreams," he finds himself transformed into a giant insect. Like Golyadkin, he feels uncertain about reality: "What has happened to me? he thought. It was no dream. His room, a regular human bedroom, only rather too small, lay quiet between the four familiar walls." Assured of his surroundings, his eyes turn next to the window, and the overcast sky and the rain make him melancholy. "What about sleeping a little longer and forgetting all this nonsense," he thinks, and tries to turn over; but he is unable to move his insect shape. The pimple, the unpleasant outgrowth from within, has breached the surface of his conscious life.

Undoubtedly, the insect metaphor came from other works by Dostoyevsky, like *Notes from the Underground*, in which another disgruntled clerk has "tried many times to become an insect;" or like *The Brothers Karamazov*, in which Dmitri characterizes the whole family as insects, or as victims of insects which live within them and govern their shameful conduct. As Kafka must have seen, the insect is the double in a different guise. In imitating the early novel, he had simply switched to the more striking metaphor and fused it with the opening scene. Of course, the imitation extends beyond this point, to the anxieties of urban life. Both heroes fear their office superiors, for example, and by turns assert and debase themselves before them; both frighten their superiors off through startling modes of illness; and both suffer from social or familial exclusion, and from their own hidden fears about sexual love. Such parallels show how Dostoyevsky set a precedent for Kafka's urban nightmares; but the most vital link is still the opening paragraph, where Kafka solves the formal problem of *The Double* with a *fait accompli*, and creates a bridge between two worlds. That it was his own formal problem, as well as Dostoyevsky's, seems evident from his frequent use of the device in later stories, and from its absence in his previous work.

So *The Double* has lent itself, importantly, to the development of modern psychological fantasy. But more relevant for the general reader, it remains a fine example of that genre even today. Consider a typical passage, in which Golyadkin admits that if anyone had wanted to turn him into a boot-rag, he might have done so with impunity; but still that rag would have been no ordinary one: it "would have had pride, would have been alive and had feelings; pride and feelings might have remained concealed deep in its filthy folds and been unable to speak for themselves, but all the same they would have been there." Like Gregor Samsa, Golyadkin is a vulnerable being, a boot-rag in the making, with pride and feeling submerged and inarticulate. Yet Dostoyevsky speaks for them, he reveals them to us, deep within the filthy folds of self-delusion, and by insisting on their presence, he creates an urban hero like ourselves. And curiously enough, in the absence of anything like the moral and religious leaven of the later novels, it is precisely this sense of humanity which gives the story its Kafkan quality, its blend of humor, horror, and compassion. As a last example, take the end of the novel, when Golyadkin is carted off to an asylum and the double runs along beside his carriage: "Hands thrust into the pockets of his green uniform trousers and with a satisfied look on his face, he kept pace with the carriage, jumping up first on one side, then on the other, and sometimes, seizing and hanging from the window frame, he would pop his head in and blow farewell kisses at Mr. Golyadkin." Meanwhile, inside the carriage, the clerk is faced with the burning eyes of his doctor, Krestyan Ivanovitch Rutenspitz, whose first name means "Christian," but whose verdict on the hero—like the father's verdict in "The Judgment"—comes "stern and dreadful as a judge's sentence."

MARK SPILKA

University of Michigan
May 1, 1958

# NOTE BY TRANSLATOR

FROM Dostoyevsky's time until our own, *The Double* has been neglected by all save scholars and critics, and no translator has offered an English version in which the merits of the original are apparent. This new translation has been made in the hope that it may win for *The Double* the recognition that Dostoyevsky thought it to deserve.

The present translation is from the generally published revised text of *The Double*, prepared by Dostoyevsky for a new edition of his works in 1866. This revision, which consisted mainly in pruning the work as first published, was executed in haste. As a result, an improved form has been achieved at the price of creating a few obscurities, particularly towards the end of the book, and notably in Klara Olsufyevna's letter, and in details connected with the elopement. The translator has rejected the idea of collating the text with the original. These faults, if such they can be called, do not arrest the reader in mid-sentence, and far from marring the author's intention, often reinforce it, by adding slightly to the already frightening inconsequence of Mr. Golyadkin's later arguments. The manner of Mr. Golyadkin's entry into Olsufy Ivanovich's courtyard at the beginning of Chapter 13 is somewhat abrupt, though not unduly so. Several puns on the name Golyadkin are lost in English, but their loss seems preferable to renaming the hero 'Mr. Poorfellow.'

## PRINCIPAL CHARACTERS IN THE STORY

| | |
|---|---|
| Yakov (Yasha) Petrovich Golyadkin | *A minor civil servant.* |
| Pyotr (Petrushka) | *His man.* |
| Krestyan Ivanovich Rutenspitz | *Medical adviser to Mr. Golyadkin.* |
| Andrey Filippovich | *Mr. Golyadkin's departmental head.* |
| Vladimir Semyonovich | *Nephew of Andrey Filippovich.* |
| Karolina Ivanovna | *A German, formerly Mr. Golyadkin's landlady.* |
| Olsufy Ivanovich Berendeyev | *A Civil Counsellor.* |
| Klara Olsufyevna | *His daughter.* |
| His Excellency | *A Civil General, Mr. Golyadkin's highest official superior, and over Andrey Filippovich.* |
| Anton Antonovich Setochkin | *The chief clerk under whom Mr. Golyadkin serves.* |
| Nestor Ignatyevich Vakhrameyev | *A colleague of Mr. Golyadkin's.* |

### NOTE

Russians have three names: Christian name, father's Christian name (patronymic), and surname. The usual form of address is by the first two names.

An intimate or familiar form of address is by a diminutive of the Christian name, e.g. Yasha, Petrushka.

Servants were commonly addressed by their patronymic.
—*Translator.*

IT was a little before eight when Yakov Petrovich Golyadkin, a minor civil servant, came to, yawned, stretched, and finally opened his eyes wide after a long night's rest. For two minutes or so he lay motionless in bed, like a man as yet uncertain whether he is awake or still asleep, whether all at present going on about him is reality or a continuation of his disordered dreams. But in a short while Mr. Golyadkin's senses began recording their usual everyday impressions more clearly. Everything looked back at him familiarly: the messy green walls of his little room, begrimed with soot and dust, his mahogany chest of drawers, his imitation mahogany chairs, the red painted table, the reddish oilcloth-covered ottoman patterned with sickly green flowers, and lastly the clothing he had hastily discarded the night before and thrown in a heap onto the ottoman. And then the foul, murky, grey autumnal day peered in at him through the dirty panes in such a sour, ill-humoured way, that Mr. Golyadkin had no longer any possible ground for doubting that he lay, not in some distant fairy realm, but in his own rooms on the fourth floor of a large tenement house in Shestilavochnaya Street, in the capital city of St. Petersburg. Having made a discovery of such importance, Mr. Golyadkin twitched his eyes shut again, as though regretting his recently-ended slumbers and wishing to recall them for a moment. But an instant later, having in all likelihood at last stumbled upon the one idea about which his scattered and inconsequent thoughts had been revolving, he bounded out of bed, and ran to a small round mirror standing on the chest or drawers. Although the sleepy, weak-sighted and rather bald image reflected was of so insignificant a character as to be certain of commanding no great attention at a first glance, its possessor remained well pleased with all that he beheld in the mirror.

'A fine thing it would be if there was something wrong with me today,' said Mr. Golyadkin under his breath.

'A fine thing if something untoward had happened, and a strange pimple had come up, or something equally unpleasant. Still, I don't look too bad. So far all's well.'

Taking a great pleasure in the fact that all was well, Mr. Golyadkin replaced the mirror, and though barefoot and still dressed in the manner in which he was accustomed to retire to bed, ran to the window and began looking intently for something in the courtyard below. What he saw was evidently also to his satisfaction, for his face lit with a self-contented smile. Then, after first peeping behind the partition into the closet occupied by his servant Petrushka, and assuring himself of his absence, he tiptoed to the table, unlocked one of the drawers, and rummaging in a far corner, finally produced from beneath some old yellow-stained papers and other rubbish a worn green note-case, carefully opened it, and looked cautiously and with manifest enjoyment into the most remote of its secret pockets. And probably the bundle of nice green, grey, blue, red and particoloured notes it contained looked up at Mr. Golyadkin with equal approval and affability, for, with face beaming, he placed the open note-case in front of him on the table, and rubbed his hands energetically in a manner betokening extreme pleasure. At last he drew out his comforting bundle of banknotes, and for the hundredth time since the day before, began counting them, rubbing each carefully between finger and thumb.

'Seven hundred and fifty roubles in notes!' he breathed finally in a half-whisper. 'Seven hundred and fifty roubles. A good sum! A pleasant sum,' he continued, his voice trembling and somewhat weakened by the emotion of his gratification, the wad of notes clenched in his hands, and his face wreathed in smiles. 'A very pleasant sum indeed! A pleasant enough sum for anyone! I'd like to see the man now who'd think it wasn't. A man can go a long way on a sum like this!'

'But what's this, where's Petrushka got to?' thought Mr. Golyadkin, and clad as he was, took another look behind the partition. Petrushka was still nowhere to be seen, but on the floor where it had been set, quite beside itself, fuming, working itself into a passion, and threatening the whole while to boil over, was the samovar; and what it was probably saying as it burred and lisped away furiously at Mr. Golyadkin in its own strange tongue was:

'Come along and fetch me, good people, I'm quite ready, you see.'

'To hell with him!' thought Mr. Golyadkin. 'That lazy lump is enough to drive a man out of his wits. Where's he disappeared to?'

Seething with righteous indignation, he went out into the hall, which consisted of a small corridor terminated by the door of the entrance, and caught sight of his servant surrounded by a whole crowd of menials and riff-raff. Petrushka was busy recounting something, the others were all attention. Clearly neither the subject of conversation nor the conversation itself were to Mr. Golyadkin's liking, for he immediately called to Petrushka, and went back into the room looking thoroughly displeased, and even disturbed.

'That wretch would betray anyone for a song, his master especially,' he thought. 'And he's betrayed me, I'm certain of that—for a miserable farthing, I wouldn't mind betting . . . Well?'

'They've brought the livery, sir.'

'Put it on, and come here.'

Having done so, Petrushka came into his master's room grinning foolishly. His costume was odd in the extreme. He was attired in green footman's livery, trimmed with gold braid and very much worn, that had obviously been intended for someone a good two feet taller. He held a hat decorated with green feathers and also trimmed with gold braid, and wore at his side a footman's sword in a leather scabbard. To complete the picture he had, following his favourite practice of going about in a homely state or undress, nothing on his feet.

Mr. Golyadkin inspected Petrushka thoroughly and seemed well pleased. Evidently the livery had been hired for some special occasion. And it was noticeable that Petrushka throughout the inspection watched his master with a strange air or expectancy, and followed his every move with unusual curiosity, much to Mr. Golyadkin's embarrassment.

'What about the carriage?'

'That's come too.'

'For the whole day?'

'Yes. Twenty-five roubles.'

'Have they brought the boots?'

'They've brought them as well.'

'Blockhead! Can't you say "Yes, they have, *sir*"?'

Having expressed his gratification at the manner in which the boots fitted, he ordered his tea and washing and shaving water to be brought. He shaved and washed with extreme care, hurriedly sipping his tea between whiles; then, setting about his final and major toilet, donned an almost new pair of trousers, a shirt front with little bronze buttons, and a waistcoat brightly adorned with nice little flowers; about his neck he tied a speckled silk cravat, and lastly pulled on a uniform jacket, carefully brushed and also nearly new. Several times while thus engaged he looked lovingly at his boots, raising first one foot then the other to admire the style, all the while muttering something to himself, and occasionally winking and making an expressive grimace as a thought occurred to him. On this particular morning however, Mr. Golyadkin was extremely preoccupied, for he scarcely noticed the grins and grimaces that Petrushka directed at him while assisting in his toilet. Finally, when he had arranged everything as it should be and was completely dressed, Mr. Golyadkin put his note-case into his pocket, took a last admiring look at Petrushka—who, having put on his boots was also quite ready—remarked that everything was done and that there was nothing to wait for, and went bustling down the stairs, his heart throbbing slightly.

A sky-blue hired carriage emblazoned with some sort of coat of arms came thundering up to

the door. Petrushka, exchanging winks with the
driver and some lounging bystanders, saw his
master seated, and in a strange voice, being scarcely
able to contain his idiotic laughter, shouted 'Drive
off!' sprang onto the rear footboard, and the whole
equipage thundered away with a crashing and
jingling in the direction of the Nevsky Prospect.

No sooner had the sky-blue carriage passed
through the gateway, than Mr. Golyadkin rubbed
his hands convulsively and shook with silent
mirth, like a merry fellow who has managed to
pull off some splendid joke, and is as pleased as
Punch about it. But immediately after this glee-
ful outburst, the laughter on Mr. Golyadkin's
face yielded to an expression that was curiously
apprehensive. In spite of the damp dismal weather,
he lowered both windows of the carriage and
began looking anxiously to left and right at the
people in the street, assuming a studied air of
decorum and sobriety immediately he noticed
anyone looking at him. At the junction of
Liteynaya Street and the Nevsky Prospect he
shuddered, having suddenly experienced a most
unpleasant sensation, and screwing up his face like
some unfortunate whose corn has been trodden
on, pressed himself hastily, and fearfully even,
into the darkest corner of his carriage. The reason
for this was that he had encountered two of his
colleagues, two young officials from the very department in which he himself was employed. It

seemed to Mr. Golyadkin that they for their part were utterly confounded at encountering him thus, and that one of them even pointed at him. It seemed that the other called him loudly by name, which was, of course, very unbecoming in the street. Our hero concealed himself, and did not respond.

'What uncouth young men!' he thought. 'What's so unusual about being in a carriage? If you need a carriage, you take one. Uncouth lot! I know them, the young hooligans. A good drubbing is what they need! Playing heads or tails with their salary and roaming the streets, that's all they're good for. I'd tell them all a thing or two . . .'

Suddenly petrified, Mr. Golyadkin left his sentence unfinished. An elegant droshky, drawn by a pair of mettlesome Kazan horses well known to Mr. Golyadkin, was rapidly overhauling his carriage on the right. The gentleman seated in the droshky, chancing to catch sight of Mr. Golyadkin's face, which the latter had rather rashly thrust out of the carriage window, seemed quite amazed at such an unlooked-for encounter, and, leaning out as far as he could, peered most interestedly and inquisitively into the very corner of the carriage in which our hero was with all haste concealing himself. The gentleman in the droshky was Andrey Filippovich, the departmental head under whom Mr. Golyadkin held the position of assistant to the chief clerk. Seeing that concealment was quite out of the question since Andrey Filippovich, having recognised him, was now staring hard at him, his eyes nearly popping out of his head, Mr. Golyadkin coloured up to the ears.

'Shall I bow? Shall I make some response? Shall I admit it's me, or shan't I?' thought our hero in indescribable anguish. 'Or shall I pretend it's not me, but someone extraordinarily like me, and just look as if nothing had happened? It really isn't me, it *isn't* me, and that's all there is to it,' said Mr. Golyadkin, raising his hat to Andrey Filippovich and not taking his eyes off him. Soon, however, the droshky overtook the carriage, bringing to an end the magnetic influence exerted by the gaze of the departmental head, but leaving Mr. Golyadkin blushing, smiling and muttering to himself.

'I was a fool not to respond,' he thought finally. 'I ought simply to have spoken up boldly, been frank and open about it. "There it is, Andrey Filippovich, I've been asked to dinner as well!"'

Then suddenly remembering that he had made a fool of himself, our hero flushed like fire, scowled and directed at the opposite corner of the carriage a look both terrible and defiant, that was intended to reduce all his enemies instantaneously to ashes. Finally, impelled by some sudden flash of inspiration, he tugged at the cord attached to the driver's elbow, stopped the carriage, and ordered the driver to turn back to Liteynaya Street. The truth was that Mr. Golyadkin had felt an immediate need, probably for his own peace of mind, to communicate something of the greatest importance to his doctor, Krestyan Ivanovich Rutenspitz. His acquaintance with the latter was admittedly of short standing, for it had been only the week before that he had visited him for the first time, on account of certain ailments. But after all, a doctor was supposed to be like a confessor, and to hide away from him would be foolish, since it was his job to know his patient.

'Will it be all right, I wonder?' pondered our hero, alighting at the entrance of a five-storeyed house in Liteynaya Street, before which he had ordered the carriage to stop.

'Is it a right and proper time to call? Well, what does it matter?' he continued, trying as he mounted the stairs to get his breath and stop his heart from throbbing, as it invariably did on other people's staircases.

'Well, what does it matter? After all, I've come on my own account. There's nothing wrong in that. It would be stupid to go hiding away. I'll just make out I didn't come for anything special, but was just passing . . . He'll see that's as it should be.'

While busy with these thoughts, Mr. Golyadkin had reached the second floor, and stopped outside Flat No. 5, which had affixed to the door a fine copper plate with the inscription:

### KRESTYAN IVANOVICH RUTENSPITZ
Physician and Surgeon

Standing before the door, our hero lost no time in assuming a countenance of due ease and affability, and prepared to pull the bell. Thus poised, he came to an immediate and rather opportune decision that it might perhaps be better to leave his visit till next day, since there was no great necessity for it at the moment. But suddenly hearing footsteps on the stairs, Mr. Golyadkin promptly reversed his new decision, and at the same time rang resolutely at Dr. Rutenspitz' bell.

## 2

D R. RUTENSPITZ, Physician and Surgeon, was an exceptionally healthy, albeit elderly gentleman, with bushy, greying eyebrows and sidewhiskers, an expressive twinkling gaze that seemed by itself to scare away all maladies, and a high decoration upon his breast. On this particular morning, he was sitting in a comfortable armchair in his consulting room, smoking a cigar, drinking coffee brought to him by his wife herself, and now and then writing prescriptions for his patients. The last draught prescribed by him had been for an old man with haemorrhoids, and now, having seen this worthy out of a side door, he was sitting awaiting the next patient.

In walked Mr. Golyadkin.

Evidently the doctor neither expected nor wished to see Mr. Golyadkin, for he was for the moment suddenly bewildered, and unwittingly allowed a strange look, one might almost say a look of annoyance, to cross his face.

As, for his part, Mr. Golyadkin somehow almost invariably turned up at the wrong time, and lost his head the moment he had occasion to approach someone on a personal matter, so now, having failed to prepare the opening sentence which was the real stumbling-block for him at such times, he grew dreadfully confused, muttered something that might have been an apology, then, being at a loss what to do next, took a chair and sat down. Suddenly recollecting that he had not been invited to do so, and sensing the impropriety of his action, he made haste to rectify this breach of social etiquette and *bon ton* by rising from the seat he had so unceremoniously taken. Gathering his wits and realising vaguely that he had committed two blunders at once, he then resolved without delay upon committing a third, that is, he attempted an apology, muttered something with a smile, grew flushed and confused, relapsed into an expressive silence, sat down again, this time for good, and protected himself against every eventuality by means of that defiant look which possessed the singular power of enabling him to reduce all his enemies to ashes and utter destruction. It was, moreover, a look that gave full expression to Mr. Golyadkin's independence, making it clear that he had nothing to worry about, that he went his own way like anyone else, and had in any case nothing to do with what concerned other people.

Dr. Rutenspitz coughed and cleared his throat, evidently as a sign that all this met with his agreement and approval, and fixed a searching inquisitorial gaze upon Mr. Golyadkin.

'Dr. Rutenspitz,' began Mr. Golyadkin, smiling, 'I have come to bother you a second time, and for a second time I venture to ask your indulgence.'

Mr. Golyadkin was obviously finding difficulty in selecting the right words.

'M-m yes,' said Dr. Rutenspitz, allowing a stream of smoke to escape from his mouth, and placing his cigar on the table. 'But you must follow my instructions, you know. I told you your treatment must take the form of a change of habits. Amuse yourself, visit your friends and acquaintances, don't grudge yourself a bottle occasionally, and keep gay company.'

Still smiling, Mr. Golyadkin was quick to remark that as he saw it he was just like anyone else; he was his own master, had his amusements just like anyone else, and naturally could go to the theatre, for like other people he had the means; he was at his post in the office during the day, but was at home in the evening; he was all right, and was, as he saw fit to observe here in passing, as well off as the next man; he had his own place, and finally he had his man Petrushka. At this point Mr. Golyadkin faltered.

'M-m-m no, that's not the sort of life at all, I wasn't meaning to ask you about that,' said the doctor. 'What I want to know is whether you are fond of gay company, whether you have a good time. Now then, are you leading a melancholy sort of life, or a gay one?'

'Dr. Rutenspitz, I . . .'

'H-m, what I'm saying,' interrupted the doctor, 'is that you must radically reform your whole life, and in a sense change your character completely.' Dr. Rutenspitz strongly emphasised the word 'change', and paused for a moment with a highly significant look.

'Don't fight shy of gay life,' he continued. 'Go to theatres, go to a club, and in any case don't be afraid of an occasional glass. It's no use staying at home. You simply mustn't.'

'I like peace and quiet,' said Mr. Golyadkin, throwing a meaning glance at the doctor, and obviously seeking the words that would best render his thoughts. 'There's no one at my place except myself and Petrushka—I mean my man, Doctor. What I mean is, Doctor, I go my own way, my own peculiar way, Doctor. I keep to myself, and so far as I can see am not dependent on anyone. Also I go for walks, Doctor.'

'What's that? . . . Yes. But there's not much pleasure in that at the moment. The weather is terrible.'

'Yes, Doctor. But as I believe I have already had the honour of explaining, although I am a quiet sort of person, my path is separate from other people's. The road of life is a broad one, Doctor . . . What I mean, what I mean to say is . . . Forgive me, Doctor, I have no gift for fine phrases.'

'M-m-m, you were saying . . .'

'I say you must forgive me, Doctor, for having so far as I can see no gift for fine phrases,' said Mr. Golyadkin in a half-offended tone, now a little lost and perplexed. 'In this respect, Doctor, I am not as other people,' he added with a peculiar sort of smile. 'I'm no great talker. I haven't learnt to embellish what I say. But to make up for it, I'm a man of action, a man of action, Doctor.'

'M-m-m . . . What's that? . . . So you're a man of action,' responded the doctor. Then for a moment there was silence, while the doctor stared in a strange and incredulous way at Mr. Golyadkin, and the latter, in turn, looked incredulously askance at the doctor.

'Peace is what I like, Doctor, not the tumult of society,' continued Mr. Golyadkin, still in his former tone, a little exasperated and bewildered by the doctor's stubborn silence. 'With most people—in society, I mean—you have to know how to bow and scrape.' (Here Mr. Golyadkin did a bow.) 'That's expected of you in society. You're asked to make puns, too, if you please, pay scented compliments, that's what's expected of you. But I haven't learnt to do this, Doctor —I haven't learnt all these cunning ways, I've had no time for them. I'm a plain simple man. There's no outward show about me. On this point, Doctor, I lay down my arms—or to continue the metaphor, I surrender.'

All this, of course, was delivered in a manner that made it quite clear that our hero had no regrets about his metaphorical surrender and his inability to acquire cunning ways, but entirely the reverse. While listening to him, the doctor, his face unpleasantly grimaced, kept his eyes upon the floor, as if preoccupied with a presentiment of some sort.

Mr. Golyadkin's tirade was followed by a rather long and significant silence. At length, in a low voice, the doctor said:

'You seem to have wandered a little off the subject. I confess I have not quite followed you.'

'I'm not one for fine phrases, Doctor,' said Mr. Golyadkin, this time in an abrupt incisive tone. 'I am not, as I have already had the honour of informing you, Doctor, one for fine phrases.'

'H-m-m!'

'Dr. Rutenspitz, when I came in, I began by apologizing. Now I repeat what I said before, and again ask your indulgence for a time.' Mr. Golyadkin began once more in a low taut expressive voice, that dwelt upon every point, and had a solemn ring about it. 'Dr. Rutenspitz, I have nothing to conceal from you. I am a little man, you know that yourself. But fortunately I have no regrets about being a little man. Quite the contrary, Doctor, and to be completely frank, I'm even proud of being a little man and not a

big one. Not being an intriguer—that's something
else I'm proud of. I don't do things on the quiet,
but openly, without a lot of artifice, and though
I could do my share of harm, and do it very well
too, and though I even know whom to harm
and how to do it, I don't sully myself with these
things, I wash my hands of them, Doctor. I wash
my hands of them, Doctor!' For a moment
Mr. Golyadkin relapsed into an expressive silence.
He had been speaking with mild enthusiasm.

'I go about straight and openly,' he continued
suddenly. 'I don't go beating about the bush,
because that's a way of doing things I scorn, and
leave to others. I don't go trying to humiliate
those who maybe are better than you or I . . .
That is, better than I, I didn't mean to say
"better than you", Doctor. I don't like odd words
here and there, miserable double-dealing I can't
stand, slander and gossip I abominate. The only
time I put on a mask is when I go to a masquerade,
I don't go about in front of people in one every
day. I will merely ask, Doctor, how *you* would
take revenge on your worst enemy, or him you
regarded as such?' concluded Mr. Golyadkin,
glancing defiantly at Dr. Rutenspitz.

But though Mr. Golyadkin had spoken throughout with the utmost clarity, precision and assur-
ance, weighing his words and relying on those
calculated to produce the best effect, he was now
looking at the doctor with ever-growing uneasiness.

He was all attention, timidly awaiting the doctor's reply with a sick uneasy feeling of impatience. But Dr. Rutenspitz, to Mr. Golyadkin's surprise and utter consternation, muttered something under his breath, pulled his chair up to the table, observed dryly, but none the less politely, something to the effect that his time was of value to him, and that somehow he did not quite follow; he was prepared to be of assistance so far as lay in his power, and to the extent of his abilities, but beyond that, into matters of no concern to him, he would not venture. At this point he took his pen, drew towards him a sheet of paper from which he cut a strip the size of a doctor's prescription, and announced that he would prescribe what was appropriate.

'No, Dr. Rutenspitz, it's not appropriate! It's not appropriate at all!' said Mr. Golyadkin rising from his seat and seizing the doctor's right hand. 'There's no need for that at all in this case!'

While he was speaking, a peculiar change came over Mr. Golyadkin. His grey eyes flashed with strange fire, his lips trembled, all his muscles and features twitched and disarranged themselves. His whole body shook violently. Having followed his first impulse in arresting the doctor's hand, Mr. Golyadkin now stood stock-still as though lacking self-assurance, and awaiting inspiration for further action.

A rather peculiar scene followed.

For the moment somewhat at a loss, Dr. Rutenspitz remained glued to his seat, and stared at Mr. Golyadkin in open-eyed amazement, while the latter stared back in the same fashion. At length the doctor rose, supporting himself to some extent by one of the lapels of Mr. Golyadkin's jacket. Thus for a few seconds they stood, motionless, not taking their eyes off one another. Then, however, followed in a most extraordinary manner Mr. Golyadkin's second impulsive action. His lips trembled, his chin quivered, and quite unexpectedly, he burst into tears. Sobbing, bobbing his head up and down, beating his breast with one hand and clutching at the lapel of Dr. Rutenspitz' coat with the other, he tried to speak, tried to offer some sort of explanation, but no words came.

Dr. Rutenspitz recovered at last from his amazement.

'That's enough of this. Calm yourself. Sit down,' he said, attempting to seat Mr. Golyadkin in the arm-chair.

'I have enemies, Doctor, I have enemies. I have deadly enemies who have sworn to ruin me . . .' replied Mr. Golyadkin in a fearful whisper.

'Enough about your enemies! No need to bring them in. No need at all. Sit down, sit down,' continued the doctor, finally getting him into the chair.

Mr. Golyadkin settled himself in the chair, not taking his eyes off the doctor, who began striding from one corner of his consulting room to the other, looking extremely displeased.

A long silence ensued.

'I'm grateful to you, Doctor, extremely grateful, and am most sensible of all that you have done for me. I shall not forget your kindness till the day I die,' said Mr. Golyadkin at length, rising from the chair with a hurt expression.

'Enough, enough, I tell you!' retorted the doctor at this sally, again forcing Mr. Golyadkin into his seat. 'What's the matter? Tell me what's upsetting you now, and who these enemies are you speak of. What's it all about?' he continued.

'No, Doctor, let's leave it at this,' answered Mr. Golyadkin, looking at the floor. 'It's best left till another time, Doctor . . . Till a more convenient time when all will be made clear, when the masks will fall from certain faces, and this and that will come to light. But meanwhile, after what has passed between us . . . You yourself will agree, Doctor . . . Allow me to wish you good morning,' said Mr. Golyadkin, rising from his seat gravely and deliberately, and reaching for his hat.

'Well, as you wish . . . H-m-m . . .' (A momentary silence.) 'For my part, you know . . . Anything I can do . . . And, er . . . I sincerely wish you all the best.'

'I understand, I understand, Doctor. I take your meaning perfectly . . . At any rate, forgive my bothering you, Doctor.'

'M-m-m no, I didn't mean that. Still, as you wish. Carry on with the medicine as before.'

'I'll carry on with the medicine as you say, Doctor. I'll carry on with it, and get it at the same chemist's . . . It's a grand thing being a chemist nowadays, Doctor . . . A grand thing.'

'Eh? In what sense?'

'In the most usual sense, Doctor. I mean that's how the world is nowadays . . .'

'H-m-m.'

'And that every little whipper-snapper—and not only in chemists' shops—looks down his nose at a gentleman.'

'H-m. How do you mean?'

'I'm speaking of someone well known, Doctor . . . A mutual friend of ours . . . Shall we say Vladimir Semyonovich, for instance?'

'Ah!'

'Yes, Doctor. And some I could name aren't so bound by what people think that they can't occasionally come out with the truth.'

'How do you mean?'

'Well, like this. It's neither here nor there, but still . . . They know how to spring the odd surprise.'

'How to what?'

'Spring a surprise, Doctor. It's a saying we've

got. They sometimes know how to pay someone a compliment that's very much to the point for instance. There are such people, Doctor.'

'Pay someone a compliment?'

'Yes, Doctor, as an intimate acquaintance of mine did the other day.'

'An intimate acquaintance of yours, eh? How was that, then?' said Dr. Rutenspitz, regarding Mr. Golyadkin attentively.

'Yes, a certain intimate acquaintance of mine was congratulating another very intimate acquaintance, who was, moreover, a close friend of mine, "a bosom friend" as the saying is, on his promotion to the rank of Assessor. The way he chanced to put it was: "I'm heartily glad of this opportunity of offering you my congratulations, my *sincere* congratulations, Vladimir Semyonovich, on your promotion—the more so since nowadays, as all the world knows, those who push their favourites are no more."' Here Mr. Golyadkin wagged his head roguishly and squinted at Dr. Rutenspitz.

'H-m. He said that, did he?'

'That's what he said, Doctor, and he looked at Andrey Filippovich, the uncle of our dear Vladimir Semyonovich. But what does it matter to me his being made an assessor? Is that any business of mine? And there he is wanting to get married and his mother's milk still wet on his lips, if you'll pardon the expression. I said as much. "There

it is Vladimir Semyonovich," I said. Now I've
told you all there is, and with your permission
I'll be getting along.'

'H-m-m.'

'Yes, Doctor, you must allow me to be getting
along, I say. But to kill two birds with one stone,
after I'd given the young man a start with that
bit about pushing favourites, I turned to Klara
Olsufyevna, who'd just been singing a tender
ballad—all this was the day before yesterday, at
her father's—and I said: "Your singing is full of
tenderness, but those who listen haven't got pure
hearts." I gave a clear hint there, you see Doctor,
a clear hint, so that they didn't take it as referring
to her, but looked further afield.'

'And what about him?'

'He looked as if he'd bitten a lemon, as the
saying is.'

'H-m-m . . .'

'Yes, Doctor, I spoke to the old man also, and
I said: "Olsufy Ivanovich," I said, "I know I am
indebted to you, and I deeply appreciate the
benefits you have lavished upon me since I was
almost a child. But open your eyes, Olsufy
Ivanovich," I said. "Take a good look around.
I myself deal frankly and openly, Olsufy Ivanovich."'

'Quite so.'

'Yes, Doctor, there it is.'

'And what did he say?'

'What did he say? He hummed and ha-ed, said this and that, about knowing me and about his Excellency's beneficence—and went all round the mulberry bush . . . But what can you expect? He's shaky with age, as they say.'

'So that's how it is now!'

'Yes, Doctor. That's how it is with all of us! Poor old chap! Already one foot in the grave and smelling of incense, as the saying is, but the moment they start some old wives' gossip, he's there to listen; they can't get on without him . . .'

'Gossip, you say?'

'Yes, Doctor, they've made up some gossip. Our friend the Bear and his dear little nephew had a hand in it. They got together with the old women, and cooked it up. And what do you think? They've thought up a plan to destroy someone.'

'Destroy someone?'

'Yes, Doctor, to destroy someone morally. They put out a rumour . . . I'm still speaking of my close friend . . .'

Dr. Rutenspitz nodded.

'They put out a rumour about him . . . I must confess, Doctor, I feel ashamed to speak of it.'

'H-m-m . . .'

'They put out a rumour saying he'd made a written promise of marriage when he was married already. And who do you think it was to, Doctor?'

'No idea.'

'A cook, a disreputable German woman who used to give him his dinner. He offered her his hand instead of payment.'

'Is that what they say?'

'Can you believe it, Doctor? A German, a vile beastly brazen German woman, Karolina Ivanovna, if you know . . .'

'For my part, I confess . . .'

'I understand you, Doctor, I quite understand, and feel it myself . . .'

'Tell me, please, where you're living now.'

'Where I'm living now, Doctor?'

'Yes . . . I wanted . . . I seem to remember you used to live . . .'

'I did, Doctor, I did, I did use to. How could I help doing so?' replied Mr. Golyadkin, accompanying his words with a short laugh.

The doctor was somewhat nonplussed by this reply.

'No, you missed my meaning. I wanted to . . .'

'So did I, Doctor, so did I . . .' continued Mr. Golyadkin with a laugh. 'But I've sat taking up too much of your time, Doctor. Pray allow me to wish you good morning.'

'H-m-m . . .'

'Yes, Doctor, I understand you. I now understand you perfectly,' said our hero, assuming a rather theatrical pose. 'And so allow me to wish you good morning.'

With this our hero bowed, and walked from the room, leaving Dr. Rutenspitz utterly amazed.

On his way down the doctor's staircase, he smiled and rubbed his hands with glee. Once on the front steps and breathing the fresh air, he felt free, and was even ready to admit himself the happiest of mortals and go straight to the office. Then suddenly his carriage came rumbling in at the gate. One look, and it all came back to him. Petrushka was already opening the carriage door. A strange, extremely unpleasant sensation seized Mr. Golyadkin's whole body. His face seemed to flush for a moment. He had a stabbing pain in his side. Just as he was about to set foot on the step of the carriage, he turned to look at Dr. Rutenspitz' windows. It was as he thought! The doctor was standing at one of them, smoothing his side-whiskers with his right hand, and gazing rather curiously at our hero.

'That doctor is stupid,' thought Mr. Golyadkin as he concealed himself in his carriage. 'Terribly stupid. He may be able to cure his patients, but he's as soft as they make them, all the same.'

Mr. Golyadkin sat back, Petrushka cried 'Drive on!' and the carriage moved out again into the Nevsky Prospect.

## 3

THIS whole morning was one of frightful
activity for Mr. Golyadkin. Once in the
Nevsky Prospect, our hero ordered the carriage
to stop at the Arcade. Jumping down, he ran in
accompanied by Petrushka, and made a bee-line
for a shop displaying gold and silver ware. From
his very appearance it was plain that Mr. Golyadkin
was a man with his hands full and a terrible amount
to get through. After settling for the purchase
of a complete tea and dinner service for one
thousand five hundred roubles, together with a
fantastically-shaped cigar-case and a complete
shaving outfit in silver for a similar sum, after
finally inquiring the price of other trifles, pleasing
and useful in their way, Mr. Golyadkin concluded by promising to return on the morrow
without fail, or even to send for his purchases that
same day, noted the number of the shop, listened
attentively while the shopkeeper solicited a small
deposit, and promised that there should indeed
be a small deposit in due course. Thereupon
he bade the stupefied shopkeeper a hurried
good-day, and pursued by a whole swarm of
assistants, made his way along the row of shops
carefully searching for somewhere new, and

turning every minute to look at Petrushka. On
the way he darted into a money changer's, and
changed his big notes into notes of smaller de-
nominations, losing on the transaction, but ac-
quiring nevertheless a great number of small
notes to swell his pocket-book, which evidently
afforded him the keenest satisfaction. At length
he stopped at a shop dealing in various ladies'
materials. Here again, after bargaining over the
purchase of goods worth a considerable sum, Mr.
Golyadkin promised the shopkeeper to return
without fail, took the number of the shop, and
the question of a small deposit being raised, repeated that there would in due course be a small
deposit. He then visited several other shops,
and in each bargained for goods and inquired
prices, sometimes having long arguments with
the shopkeepers and walking out only to come
back three times afterwards—in short, he showed
unusual activity. From the Arcade our hero
betook himself to a well-known furnisher's, where
he ordered furniture for six rooms, and admired
an intricately designed ladies' dressing-table in the
latest style. After assuring the shopkeeper that he
would send for it all without fail, he left the shop
with his customary promise of a small deposit,
and drove off to order something else. To put
it briefly, there seemed no end to his activity.

At last Mr. Golyadkin seemed to grow sick and
tired of it all, and even began, heaven knows why,

to be troubled by twinges of conscience. Nothing
on earth would have induced him to meet Andrey
Filippovich or Dr. Rutenspitz for instance.

Finally the city clocks struck three, and as Mr.
Golyadkin got back into his carriage, a pair of
gloves and a bottle of perfume for one and a half
roubles represented all that he had actually
purchased.

As he was still rather early, Mr. Golyadkin
ordered the driver to stop at a well-known
restaurant in the Nevsky Prospect which so far
he had known only by repute. He jumped down
and hurried in to have a bite to eat and take his
ease till the appointed time.

After eating as befits a man with the prospect
of a sumptuous dinner-party before him—that is,
having snatched the odd something to stay the
pangs as the saying is, and swallowed a glass of
vodka—Mr. Golyadkin settled himself in an arm-
chair, and after a discreet look round, quietly
attached himself to a certain meagre national
newspaper. After reading a few lines he rose,
looked at himself in the mirror, righted his dress
and smoothed his hair; after which he went to
the window to see if his carriage was there, then
resumed his seat and took up the newspaper.
Our hero was clearly in a state of extreme agitation. Glancing at the clock, and seeing that as
it was only a quarter past three there was still
some time to wait, Mr. Golyadkin decided that

it was not proper just to sit there, and ordered a chocolate that he did not particularly want. After drinking the chocolate and noting that the time had got on a bit, Mr. Golyadkin went to pay his bill. Suddenly someone clapped him on the shoulder.

He turned and saw before him his two office colleagues, the two fellows young in years and junior in rank, whom he had met that morning in Liteynaya Street. Our hero was on no particular footing with them, was neither friendly nor openly hostile towards them. Correctness, of course, was observed on both sides, but nothing further. Indeed, there could be nothing further. The present encounter was disagreeable to Mr. Golyadkin in the extreme. He frowned slightly and was for the moment embarrassed.

'Yakov Petrovich, Yakov Petrovich!' twittered the two clerks. 'You here? What brings you . . .?'

'Oh, it's you, gentlemen,' interposed Mr. Golyadkin hurriedly, somewhat disconcerted and scandalized by the clerks' surprise at seeing him, and by their familiarity, but pretending despite himself to be a free and easy sort of fellow. 'So you've deserted the office, eh? Ha-ha-ha!' And here, to preserve his dignity and patronize the office juniors, from whom he always kept his proper distance, he tried to tap one of the young men on the shoulder. But on this occasion the popular approach failed Mr. Golyadkin, and instead of his making a seemly, intimate gesture, something quite different happened.

'Well, is our old Bear still sitting there?' he blurted out.

'Who do you mean, Yakov Petrovich?'

'Come, come. As if you didn't know!'

Mr. Golyadkin gave a laugh, and turned to collect his change. 'I'm speaking of Andrey Filippovich, gentlemen,' he continued, when he had finished with the cashier, now addressing the clerks with a very earnest expression. The two clerks exchanged knowing winks.

'He's still there, Yakov Petrovich, and he was asking for you.'

'He is, eh? Well, let him stay there, gentlemen. And so he was asking for me, was he?'

'Yes, he was, Yakov Petrovich. But what's all this perfume and pomade? You're the real dandy.'

'Yes, that's how it is gentlemen. But enough ——' replied Mr. Golyadkin looking away with a forced smile. Seeing him smiling, the clerks burst out laughing. Mr. Golyadkin pouted.

'I'll tell you something as a friend, gentlemen,' he said after a short silence, as if he had made a momentous decision to confide in the clerks. 'You all know me, gentlemen, but up to now you have only known one side of me. No one can be reproached for this, and I confess I am partly to blame.' Mr. Golyadkin pursed his lips and looked at the clerks significantly. The clerks again winked at each other.

'Up to the present you have not really known me, gentlemen. To explain here and now would not be at all appropriate. I'll merely give you a hint in passing. There are people, gentlemen, who don't like beating about the bush, and mask themselves only to go to a masquerade. There are people who don't see that man's one purpose in life is to be adept at bowing and scraping. There are people who don't say they're happy and enjoying life to the full just because their trousers fit well, for instance. And finally there are people who don't like leaping and whirling around when there's no need, fawning, making eyes, and, what's most important of all, gentlemen, poking their noses in where they're not asked. I have said practically all there is, gentlemen. Now, if you will allow me, I must be off.' He paused, and the clerks, having had their money's worth, burst suddenly and in a most discourteous manner into a great roar of laughter. Mr. Golyadkin flushed red with anger.

'Go on, laugh, gentlemen, laugh for the time being. You'll see when you're a bit older,' he said with injured pride, taking his hat and retiring towards the door. 'But I'll tell you something else, gentlemen,' he added, turning to the clerks for the last time. 'I'll tell you something else now we're all here face to face. My rule gentlemen,

is, if at first I don't succeed, I take courage. If I
do succeed, I hold on, and in any case I don't try
undermining anyone. I'm not one for intrigue,
and I'm proud of it. As a diplomat I'd be no good
at all. "The bird flies to the huntsman," they say,
gentlemen. That's true, I'm ready to admit.
But who's the huntsman here, and who the bird?
That's another question, gentlemen.'

Mr. Golyadkin lapsed into an eloquent silence,
and making a most expressive face, that is, raising
his eyebrows and pursing his lips as tightly as
possible, he raised his hat to the clerks and walked
out, leaving them dumbfounded.

'Where to?' asked Petrushka rather grimly,
having probably grown fed up with hanging
about in the cold. 'Where to?' he asked Mr.
Golyadkin, and met that fearful all-annihilating
glare with which our hero had already protected
himself on two occasions that morning, and to
which he now had recourse a third time while
descending the steps.

'The Izmaylovsky Bridge.'

'The Izmaylovsky Bridge!' ordered Petrushka.

'They don't begin dinner till after four, or
perhaps not till five,' thought Mr. Golyadkin.
'Isn't it a bit too early now? Still, I can arrive a
bit early. After all, it's a family dinner. I can just
go along *sans façon*, as the saying is in the best
circles. The Bear said it would all be *sans facon*,
so that goes for me too.'

Such were Mr. Golyadkin's thoughts, but meanwhile his agitation was increasing every minute. He was evidently preparing himself for something extremely troublesome, to say the least. He was whispering to himself, gesticulating with his right hand, and gazing incessantly out of the carriage window, so that no one seeing him then would have said that he was on his way to dine informally as one of the family, or *sans façon* as the saying is in the best circles.

At last, just by the Izmaylovsky Bridge, Mr. Golyadkin indicated a house, and the carriage thundered in at a gate to stop by some steps on the right. Noticing the figure of a woman in one of the second-floor windows, Mr. Golyadkin blew her a kiss. But he had no idea what he was doing, for at that moment he was neither dead nor alive, but somewhere in between. He emerged from the carriage, pale and distracted, climbed the steps to the entrance, removed his hat, straightened his clothes mechanically, and with a slight trembling at the knees made his way up the stairs.

'Is Olsufy Ivanovich at home?' he inquired of the servant who opened to him.

'Yes sir—that is, no sir. He's not at home, sir.'

'Eh? What do you mean, my dear chap? I've come to dinner, my friend. You know me, don't you?'

'Of course, sir. But my orders are not to admit you.'

'Y-y-you must be making some mistake, my friend. It's me. I've been invited. I've come to dinner,' said Mr. Golyadkin, discarding his overcoat, and showing every intention of going in.

'I'm sorry, it's no good, sir. Orders are to refuse you admittance. That's how it is.'

Mr. Golyadkin turned pale. At that moment the door of one of the inner rooms opened, and Gerasimych, Olsufy Ivanovich's old butler, appeared.

'There's a gentleman here trying to get in, and I . . .' said the servant.

'You're a fool, Alexeich. Go along and fetch that scoundrel Semyonych here.' Then turning to Mr. Golyadkin he said politely but firmly: 'It's impossible, sir. Out of the question. The master begs you to excuse him. He cannot receive you.'

'Did he say he couldn't receive me?' asked Mr. Golyadkin with a note of uncertainty. 'Excuse my asking, Gerasimych, but why is it impossible?'

'Quite impossible, sir. I announced you, and he said: "Ask him to excuse me. I cannot receive him," he said.'

'But why?'

'I'm sorry, sir.'

'But what's the reason? It's impossible! Go and announce me . . . How's it happened like this? I've come to dinner.'

'I'm sorry, sir, I'm sorry . . .'

'Ah well, if he begs to be excused, it's a different matter. But tell me, Gerasimych, why is it?'

'Excuse me, excuse me, sir!' exclaimed Gerasimych, firmly pushing Mr. Golyadkin to one side to make room for two gentlemen who were at that moment entering the hall. It was Andrey Filippovich and his nephew Vladimir Semyonovich. Both looked in a puzzled way at Mr. Golyadkin. Andrey Filippovich was on the point of saying something, but Mr. Golyadkin's mind was made up, and with eyes lowered, scarlet-faced, smiling, and looking thoroughly confused, he was already on his way out.

'I'll come back later, Gerasimych. I'll explain. I hope all this won't cause any delay in clearing things up in good time,' he said, beginning in the doorway and finishing on the stairs.

'Yakov Petrovich, Yakov Petrovich . . .' came the voice of Andrey Filippovich hard behind him.

Mr. Golyadkin was then already on the first landing. He turned quickly to face Andrey Filippovich.

'What can I do for you, Andrey Filippovich?' he said in a fairly resolute tone.

'What's the matter with you, Yakov Petrovich? How is it that . . .'

'Nothing, Andrey Filippovich. I'm here on my own account. This is my private life, Andrey Filippovich.'

'What's all that?'

'I say that this is my private life, and that regarding my official relationships, nothing reprehensible is, so far as I can see, to be found in my presence here.'

'How do you mean, "Regarding your official . . ." What's the matter with you, sir?'

'Nothing, Andrey Filippovich, nothing at all. A miserable cheeky girl, nothing else . . .'

'What! What!' Andrey Filippovich was utterly perplexed.

Mr. Golyadkin, who so far had carried on the conversation from the foot of the stairs, looked as if he were about to fly at Andrey Filippovich's face, and now, seeing the confusion of his departmental head, he almost unconsciously took a step forward. Andrey Filippovich drew back. Mr. Golyadkin moved up one stair, then another . . . Andrey Filippovich looked round uneasily. Suddenly and with great rapidity Mr. Golyadkin bounded to the head of the stairs. With even greater rapidity Andrey Filippovich sprang back into the room, slamming the door after him.

Mr. Golyadkin was alone. There was a mist before his eyes. He was completely bewildered, and stood vacant and hesitant, as though calling to mind some very stupid event that had recently occurred. 'Ah well,' he murmured, forcing a smile. In the meantime footsteps and voices had become audible on the stairs below, heralding in all probability the arrival of other of Olsufy Ivanovich's invited guests. Mr. Golyadkin came partially to his senses, and quickly turning up the racoon collar of his overcoat and concealing as much of himself as possible behind it, stumbled awkwardly downstairs as fast as his legs would carry him. He felt weak and numb inside, and his confusion was such, that on emerging from the door, he made his way straight across the muddy courtyard to his carriage, instead of waiting for it to draw up. As he prepared to climb in, Mr. Golyadkin felt as if every living soul in Olsufy Ivanovich's house was staring at him from every window, and wished inwardly that he might sink through the ground or disappear into a mouse-hole, carriage and all. If he turned round he knew he would fall dead on the spot.

'What are you laughing at, blockhead?' he fired at Petrushka.

'I'm not. What have I got to laugh about? Where to now?'

'Home.'

'Home, driver!' yelled Petrushka, perching himself on the backboard.

'He's got a voice like a crow,' thought Mr. Golyadkin.

The carriage was already some way beyond the Izmaylovsky Bridge, when suddenly our hero pulled the cord with all his might and shouted to the driver to turn back immediately. The driver turned the horses, and two minutes later they were again driving into Olsufy Ivanovich's courtyard.

'No, you fool, back again!' screamed Mr. Golyadkin, and it was as if the driver had been expecting such an order, for without either stopping or offering a word of protest, he drove the whole way round the courtyard and out again into the street.

But Mr. Golyadkin did not drive home. As soon as they had passed the Semyonovsky Bridge, he ordered the driver to turn into a side street and stop outside a rather unpretentious-looking restaurant. Once our hero had alighted he paid off the driver, and so was finally rid of his carriage. Telling Petrushka to walk home and await his return, he went into the restaurant, took a private room, and ordered dinner to be served. He felt extremely unwell, and his head seemed in a state of chaos. For a long while he paced the room in agitation. Then at last he sat down, propped his forehead on his hands, and began striving with all his might to think things out and get something settled with regard to his present position.

## 4

THE day—that festal day whereon occurred the anniversary of the birth of Klara Olsufyevna, only daughter of Civil Counsellor Berendeyev, sometime benefactor of Mr. Golyadkin, was marked by a dinner, splendid, magnificent, and such as has not been witnessed within the walls ot any civil servant's apartment in or about the neighbourhood of the Izmaylovsky Bridge for many a day; a dinner that was more like Belshazzar's Feast, there being something Babylonian about its effulgence, sumptuosity and sense of the occasion; a dinner with Veuve Clicquot, with oysters, with the fruits of Yeliseyev's and Malyutins',* with every kind of fatted calf, and an official programme setting forth the rank of each diner. The festal day signalized by so fine a dinner ended with a brilliant ball—a small, intimate, family ball, but brilliant none the less for its good taste, polish and seemliness. Such balls do, I concede, take place, but they are a rare phenomenon. Resembling as they do more joyful family occasions than anything else, they can only be given in a house such as Civil Counsellor Berendeyev's. I will go even further and say

* Fashionable St. Petersburg stores.—*Translator.*

that not every civil counsellor could give such balls.

Would I were a poet! A Homer or a Pushkin, of course, for with a lesser talent one would not attempt it—and then I would boldly and vividly depict for my readers the whole of that supremely festal day. Or rather, my poem would open with the dinner, and I should lay particular emphasis on that striking and triumphant moment of the raising of the first goblet to the health of the Queen of Festivities. I should depict the guests plunged in reverentially expectant silence—a silence of almost Demosthenian eloquence. I should then describe Andrey Filippovich, as most senior among the guests, having with his venerable grey hairs and the orders appropriate to them upon his breast some claim to precedence, rising from his seat, and holding aloft a goblet of a sparkling vintage—no common wine, but nectar —conveyed hither from a distant realm expressly to be tasted at moments such as these. I should depict for you the happy parents of the Queen of Festivities, and the guests, raising their goblets after Andrey Filippovich, and gazing at him, filled with expectancy. Then I should depict for you that same Andrey Filippovich, of whom frequent mention is made, shedding a tear into his champagne glass, delivering a speech of felicitation, and proposing and drinking the health of Klara Olsufyevna. But I must confess, and confess freely, that it would be beyond my powers to depict the full pageantry of the moment in which the Queen of Festivities, flushed like a rose of spring with the bloom of blissful modesty, sinks for excess of joy into the arms of her loving mother; how her loving mother lets fall a tear; and how at this, that venerable old man, her father Olsufy Ivanovich, who has lost the use of his legs in long service, and has for his zeal been rewarded by fate with a little capital, a small house, some small estates and a beautiful daughter, begins sobbing like a child and proclaims through his tears the beneficence of his Excellency. I should be quite unable to depict for you the general heartfelt enthusiasm which promptly ensues, and which finds eloquent expression in the behaviour of a junior clerk who in listening to Andrey Filippovich sheds a few tears of his own—looking for the moment more like a civil counsellor than a humble junior. Andrey Filippovich at this moment of triumph does not look at all like a collegiate counsellor and head of a section in a certain department. No, indeed . . . In some way he is different. I do not quite know in what way he is different, but certainly he is unlike a collegiate counsellor. He is more exalted! And finally . . . Oh, why do I not possess the secret of elevated, forceful style—of an exultant style, to depict all these beautiful and edifying moments of mortal existence, contrived as it were expressly

in evidence of the fact that virtue will sometimes
triumph over vice, envy, free-thinking and evil
intent! I will say nothing, but will point out to
you in silence—for this will be better than eloquence—that fortunate young man entering upon
his twenty-sixth year, Vladimir Semyonovich,
nephew of Andrey Filippovich, who has in turn
risen, and is in turn proposing a toast, while upon
him rest the tearful eyes of the parents of the
Queen of Festivities, the proud eyes of Andrey
Filippovich, the modest eyes of the Queen herself,
the rapturous eyes of the guests, and the decorously envious eyes of certain colleagues of this
brilliant young man. I will say nothing, although
I cannot help observing that everything about
this young man—who, let it be said in his favour,
is more like an old man than a young one—
everything, from his rosy cheeks to the rank of
Assessor with which he is invested, speaks at this
triumphant moment of the lofty heights to which
one may be elevated by good manners! I shall
not describe how finally Anton Antonovich
Setochkin, the chief clerk of a certain department,
a colleague of Andrey Filippovich, and a former
colleague of Olsufy Ivanovich, as well as being
an old friend of the family and godfather to
Klara Olsufyevna, an old man as grey as a badger,
while proposing a toast, crows like a cock and
speaks some jolly verses; and how by this decorous breach of decorum, if one may use such a

phrase, he sets the whole company laughing till the tears run, and Klara Olsufyevna, on instructions from her parents, rewards his mirth and amiability with a kiss.

I shall merely state that the guests, feeling as guests naturally must after such a dinner, rose at last from the table, brothers and bosom friends. The older and more staid gentlemen, after a short while spent in friendly conversation and the exchange of eminently decorous and amiable confidences, proceeded sedately to another room, where, breaking up into parties, they lost no time in seating themselves with proper dignity at the green baize-covered tables. The ladies, once seated in the drawing-room, suddenly became unusually amiable, and started chatting about various materials. The esteemed master of the house, who had lost the use of his legs in true and faithful service, and been recompensed for this by all that I have mentioned above, hobbled amongst his guests on crutches, supported by his daughter and Vladimir Semyonovich—when suddenly, also waxing unusually amiable, he resolved upon improvising a modest little ball, regardless of expense. To this end a bright young man—the one who at dinner looked more like a civil counsellor—was dispatched to summon musicians. The musicians arrived, eleven strong, and at last, at half past eight precisely, came the inviting strains of a French quadrille. Various other dances followed . . .

I need hardly mention that a fitting description of this ball improvised by the singular amiability of the grey-haired host is beyond the powers of my feeble pen. How can I, the humble chronicler of the adventures of Mr. Golyadkin, which are, however, very curious in their way, depict this singular and seemly medley of beauty, brilliance, decorum, gaiety, amiable sobriety and sober amiability, sprightliness and joy; depict all the playfulness and laughter of the functionaries' daughters and wives, who, and I mean this as a compliment, are more like fairies than ladies, with their pink and lily-white shoulders and faces, their slender waists, their lively, twinkling, and —to use a grand word—*homoeopathic* feet? How, finally, can I depict for you the brilliant civil service cavaliers, both stolid and gay—level-headed young men, both merry and decorously melancholy—some smoking pipes in intervals between dances in a remote small green room, others not smoking; cavaliers of proper rank and good family to a man; cavaliers deeply imbued with a sense of elegance and of their own worth; who converse with the ladies for the most part in French, but who, when speaking Russian, employ only the very best expressions, pay compliments, and voice profundities; cavaliers who only in the smoking-room permit themselves an occasional amiable departure from language of the highest tone, in phrases of amicable, good-

natured intimacy after the style of: 'You stepped
a pretty fine polka, Petka my boy!' or 'Vasya,
you old so-and-so, you gave your little lady a
jolly rough time of it!'

All this, as I have informed the reader earlier,
is beyond the power of my pen, and therefore I
remain silent. Let us rather return to Mr. Golyadkin, the true hero of my veracious tale.

His present position was curious to say the least.
He also was there, ladies and gentlemen—not *at*
the ball, that is, but very nearly. He was quite all
right, and going his own way—although for the
moment he had chosen anything but a direct
route. He was standing—it's a funny thing to
have to say—on a landing on the back stairs of
Olsufy Ivanovich's apartment. But there was
nothing wrong with his standing there. He was
quite all right. He was pressed into a corner
where, if it was not particularly warm, it was at
least as dark as possible, and he was partially
hidden, amidst all kinds of lumber and rubbish,
by an enormous cupboard and some old screens.
Here he was concealing himself until the appointed hour, and meanwhile merely following
the general course of things as an outside observer.
He was just watching . . . He could go in if he
wanted . . . After all, why shouldn't he? A few
steps, and in he'd go, with all the ease in the
world. It was only after he had been standing
between the cupboard and screens amidst all kinds

of lumber and rubbish for over two hours in the cold, that to justify himself he quoted a phrase of the late lamented French Minister Villèle, to the effect that all comes in due season to him who wisely waits. It was a phrase he'd seen some time before in a book on some quite extraneous subject, but to have recalled it at that moment was particularly appropriate. In the first place it was a phrase well-suited to his position, and, secondly, why shouldn't it have occurred to someone who had spent nearly three hours on a cold dark landing, waiting for a happy ending to his troubles? Immediately following this appropriate quotation, Mr. Golyadkin for some unknown reason called to mind the late Turkish Vizier Martsimiris and the lovely Margravine Luise, both of whom he had read about at some time or other in a book. He then called to mind that the Jesuits had a maxim that all means were justified, provided the end was attained. A little encouraged by this historical fact, he asked himself what the Jesuits were. Numskulls, every one of them! He'd outshine the lot. And if only the buffet—a door of which opened onto the back stairs and Mr. Golyadkin's landing—were clear of people for a minute, Jesuits or no Jesuits, he'd march straight through—through the tea *salon*, through the room where they were playing cards, and into the ball-room where at that moment they were dancing a polka. He'd march straight

through, in spite of everything . . . Just slip past.
No one would notice. And once there he would
know what to do.

Such, ladies and gentlemen, is the position in
which we discover the hero of our very true story.
Although to explain exactly what had been happening to him is difficult.

He had been able to get as far as the stairs and
landing, for the simple reason that everyone else
had, and he didn't see why he shouldn't too.
But go farther, he dare not—that was clear.
Not because he wouldn't, but because he didn't
want to, because he preferred to stay quiet. And
there he was, staying quiet just as he had been for
the past two and a half hours. But why shouldn't
he? Villèle waited.

'But what's Villèle got to do with it?' thought
Mr. Golyadkin. 'Why drag him in? Supposing . . . Supposing I marched in now?'

'A walking-on part—that's all you've got!'
said Mr. Golyadkin, pinching his numbed cheek
with his numbed fingers. 'What a poor stupid
fool you are!'

These blandishments were merely by the way,
and served no apparent purpose. Mr. Golyadkin
was about to intrude, and had already started forward. The time had come. The buffet was clear.
He could see that through a tiny window. Two
steps, and he was at the door and already opening
it.

'Shall I, or shan't I? Shall I?... Yes, I will—
why shouldn't I? The brave go where they please!'
Thus reassuring himself, our hero suddenly and
quite unexpectedly withdrew behind the screen.

'No,' he thought. 'Suppose someone comes
in? There you are—now someone has. Why did
I stand gaping when no one was there? Gone
straight in—that's what I ought to have done!
But what's the good of saying that when you're
made like me? It's a vile tendency I've got!
I simply went into a blue funk. That's me all
over! Always making a hash of it—no question
of that. And here I am standing round like a
blinking idiot! I could be at home now drinking
a cup of tea... A cup of tea would be jolly nice.
Petrushka will grumble if I'm late. Why not go
home? To hell with all this! Come on, I'm off!'

Having settled things thus, Mr. Golyadkin
shot forward as if a spring had been touched off
inside him. Two strides, and he was in the buffet.
Flinging off his hat and coat and stuffing them
hurriedly into a corner, he straightened his jacket,
smoothed his hair, and proceeded to the tea
*salon*. From there he whisked on into the next
room, slipped unobserved between the card-
players absorbed in the excitement of their game,
and then... At this point Mr. Golyadkin became
oblivious of all that was going on around, and
suddenly, like a bolt from the blue, he entered
the ball-room.

As if to spite him, no one was dancing. The ladies were promenading in picturesque groups. The men were gathering in little knots, or darting about engaging partners. Mr. Golyadkin noticed none of this. All he saw was Klara Olsufyevna, and standing near her, Andrey Filippovich, Vladimir Semyonovich, two or three officers, and two or three other very interesting young men who, as one could judge at first sight, were also the subject or the embodiment of great hopes. He saw one or two other people as well. Or rather—he didn't. He was no longer aware of anybody. Propelled by the same spring that had brought him bounding into a ball to which he had not been invited, he continued to advance steadily. He collided with a counsellor and trod heavily on his foot; he stepped on the dress of a certain venerable old lady and tore it slightly; he jostled a man with a tray; he elbowed somebody else, but still forged on, noticing none of this, or, more accurately, *noticing* it, but not looking at anyone, until suddenly he found himself face to face with Klara Olsufyevna. At that moment there's not a shadow of doubt he would have dropped through the floor with the greatest pleasure in the world, and without so much as blinking. But what's done can't be undone—it's quite impossible. What *could* be done?

'If at first you don't succeed, hold on. If you do succeed, take courage,' thought Mr. Golyadkin.

He was, of course, not one for intrigue—no adept at bowing and scraping . . . It had happened now. Added to which the Jesuits were mixed up in it somehow . . . But Mr. Golyadkin had no time for them! Suddenly, as though at the wave of a hand, all noise, movement, conversation and laughter ceased, and gradually a crowd formed around him. But he seemed to hear and see nothing. He couldn't look . . . He merely stood there, keeping his eyes glued to the ground, but secretly vowing on his word of honour that somehow or other he'd blow his brains out that very night.

'Here goes!' thought Mr. Golyadkin after this, and suddenly, to his own infinite astonishment, he began to speak.

Mr. Golyadkin opened with felicitations and seemly good wishes. The former went well, but over the latter he stumbled. He had sensed that if he once stumbled everything would immediately go to the devil. And so it did. Having stumbled, he got stuck. Having got stuck, he blushed. Having blushed, he became confused. Becoming confused he raised his eyes, looked about him—and froze with horror. They were all standing, speechless and expectant. A little way off someone began to whisper. Nearer at hand there was a sudden boisterous laugh. Mr. Golyadkin glanced, humbly embarrassed, at Andrey Filippovich. Andrey Filippovich retaliated with a look which would have crushed our hero completely, had he not been completely crushed already.

'This concerns more my private life and my personal affairs, Andrey Filippovich,' said Mr. Golyadkin, more dead than alive, in a voice that was barely audible. 'It's not an official matter.'

'You ought to be ashamed, sir!' said Andrey Filippovich in a half-whisper, with a look of indescribable indignation on his face, taking Klara Olsufyevna by the arm and turning away from Mr. Golyadkin.

'I've nothing to be ashamed about, Andrey Filippovich,' replied Mr. Golyadkin, also in a half-whisper, confused, and looking unhappily around in an attempt to find his milieu and proper sphere in that bewildered crowd.

'It's nothing, nothing, gentlemen. Why, it could happen to anyone,' whispered Mr. Golyadkin, shifting his position slightly in an attempt to extricate himself from the encircling throng. Way was made for him, and with difficulty our hero passed between the two rows of puzzled and curious spectators. Fate was drawing him on— he could feel it. Certainly he'd have given a great deal if without any breach of decorum, he could at that moment have found himself back on the landing. Since, however, this was quite impossible, he tried to slip into some corner where he could just stand, modest, decorous, and independent, annoying no one, calling no particular attention to himself, but at the same time finding favour with both host and guests. But Mr. Golyadkin felt as if the ground were being washed away beneath him—felt as though he were swaying and falling. He reached a corner at last, and stood there in the manner of a rather indifferent outside observer, resting his hands on the backs of two chairs to assert full possession of them, and attempting as far as possible to give those of Olsufy Ivanovich's guests who had grouped themselves around him a jaunty look. Standing closest to him was an officer, a fine tall figure of a man beside whom Mr. Golyadkin felt like something out of a cheese.

'Both these chairs are taken, Lieutenant. One is for Klara Olsufyevna, the other is for the Princess Chevchekhanova, who is dancing here. I'm keeping them for them,' said Mr. Golyadkin breathlessly, looking beseechingly at the lieutenant. The lieutenant gave him a withering smile and turned away without a word. Having suffered a rebuff in one quarter, our hero set about trying his luck elsewhere, and straightway addressed a certain pompous-looking counsellor wearing about his neck the cross of an important decoration. But the counsellor measured him with a stare that was like a sudden drenching tubful of icy water. Mr. Golyadkin fell silent. He decided it was better not to start up conversation, but to hold his peace and show that he was all right, that he was like anyone else, and that his position, as far as he could see, was at all events a proper one. To this end he glued his eyes to the cuffs of his jacket, then raised and fixed them upon a certain gentleman of extremely venerable appearance.

'This gentleman is wearing a wig,' thought Mr. Golyadkin. 'And if it's taken off, his head will be just like a billiard ball.'

After making this important discovery, Mr. Golyadkin thought of Arab emirs, and the green turbans they wear to symbolize their kinship with the prophet Mohammed. Remove the turbans and there'll also be nothing but bare, hairless heads. Then, probably by a peculiar association of ideas, Mr. Golyadkin got on to Turkish slippers, apropos of which he at once remembered that the boots Andrey Filippovich was wearing were more like slippers than boots. Clearly he was to some extent familiar with his situation.

'That chandelier up there,' flashed through Mr. Golyadkin's mind—'supposing it broke from its fittings and fell on the company—I'd rush and save Klara Olsufyevna at once. When I'd saved her I'd say: "Don't worry, young lady—it's nothing. I'm your rescuer." Then . . .' Here Mr. Golyadkin gave a sidelong glance to see where Klara Olsufyevna was, and caught sight of Gerasimych, Olsufy Ivanovich's old butler, making straight for him, with an imposingly official look of concern on his face. An unaccountable and at the same time most unpleasant sensation made Mr. Golyadkin shudder and pucker up his face. Mechanically he looked around. He had thoughts of quietly edging himself out of harm's way, and merging in with the background, that is, of acting as if nothing whatever was the matter, and he wasn't concerned in it at all. Before he could reach any decision, however, there was Gerasimych, standing in front of him.

'Can you see that candle in the candelabra, Gerasimych?' said our hero, smiling slightly. 'It's going to fall in a minute. Just go and tell someone to put it right. I'm sure it'll fall . . .'

'The candle, sir? Oh no, sir, that's all right. But there's someone asking for you, sir.'

'Who's asking for me, Gerasimych?'

'I don't know exactly, sir. It's someone with a message. "Is Yakov Petrovich here?" he said. "Then call him," he said—"it's something very vital and urgent . . ."'

'No, Gerasimych, you're mistaken, quite mistaken.'

'Hardly, sir.'

'There's no "hardly" about it! No one is asking for me, there's no one to ask. And I'm quite at home here—that is, I'm where I belong.'

Mr. Golyadkin paused for breath, and looked around. It was as he thought! Every living soul in the room was watching, listening and solemnly waiting. The men were crowding closer, all ears. Further off, the ladies were exchanging alarmed whispers. The host himself was no great distance from Mr. Golyadkin, and though he gave no indication of the direct and immediate interest he too was taking in the latter's affairs—for the whole thing was being conducted with delicacy —Mr. Golyadkin distinctly felt that the decisive moment had come. He clearly perceived that the hour for a bold stroke and the humiliation of his enemies was at hand. He was agitated. He felt a kind of sudden inspiration, and in a quavering but solemn voice he again addressed the waiting Gerasimych.

'No, my friend, no one is asking for me. You are mistaken. I will go further—you were mistaken this afternoon in giving me to understand— in *daring* to give me to understand, I say', (Mr. Golyadkin raised his voice) 'that Olsufy Ivanovich, who has been my benefactor for as long as I can remember, and who, in a certain sense, has been a father to me, had forbidden me his house at a time when his paternal heart was filled with family exultation.' (Well satisfied with himself, but deeply moved, Mr. Golyadkin looked about him. Tears started to his eyes.) 'I repeat, my friend,' concluded our hero, 'you were mistaken—cruelly and unpardonably mistaken.'

It was a moment of triumph. Mr. Golyadkin felt he had produced exactly the right effect, and

stood, eyes modestly averted, awaiting Olsufy
Ivanovich's embrace. There were clear signs of
excitement and bewilderment amongst the guests.
Even the formidable and unshakable Gerasimych
stuttered over his 'Hardly, sir . . .' Then suddenly, for no apparent reason, the unpitying
orchestra struck up a polka. All was lost—thrown
to the winds. Mr. Golyadkin shuddered. Gerasimych took a step back. The whole ball-room
surged like the sea, and there was Vladimir
Semyonovich sweeping off Klara Olsufyevna in
the first couple, followed by the splendid lieutenant
and the Princess Chevchekhanova in the second.
Onlookers, filled with curiosity and delight,
thronged to take a peep at the dancers—the polka
being a fashionable new dance that was all the
rage. Mr. Golyadkin was temporarily forgotten.
But suddenly there was general alarm and per-
turbation. The music stopped . . . Something
odd had happened.

Fatigued by the dance and almost breathless,
Klara Olsufyevna, her cheeks glowing and her
breast heaving, had sunk exhausted into an arm-
chair. All hearts had gone out to that delightful
enchantress. Everyone was vying with everyone
else to salute her and thank her for the pleasure
she had afforded them, when suddenly—there was
Mr. Golyadkin. He was pale, extremely ill at
ease, and he too seemed to be in a state of exhaustion, for he could hardly walk. For some reason

or other he was smiling and extending an inviting hand. Failing in her amazement to withdraw her hand in time, Klara Olsufyevna rose mechanically to Mr. Golyadkin's invitation. Mr. Golyadkin took one tottering step forward, then a second. He raised one foot, did a sort of bow, gave a sort of stamp, and stumbled. He too wanted to dance with Klara Olsufyevna.

Klara Olsufyevna screamed. Everyone rushed to free her hand from Mr. Golyadkin's, and in a flash our hero was pushed almost a dozen yards away by the crowd. A small group formed around him. There were cries and shrieks from two old ladies whom Mr. Golyadkin had nearly bowled over in his retreat. The confusion was appalling. Everyone was shouting, arguing and questioning his neighbour. The orchestra had fallen silent. Turning round inside the small circle of people, and half smiling, Mr. Golyadkin was mechanically muttering under his breath something about: why shouldn't he? The polka was, as far as he could see, a novel and extremely interesting dance, contrived to delight the ladies . . . But if this was how it had turned out, he was prepared to acquiesce.

But Mr. Golyadkin's acquiescence was, it seemed, not asked for. A hand fell on his arm, another descended lightly on his back, and he felt himself being steered with especial care in a certain direction.

He noticed at last that he was heading straight for the door. He thought of trying to do or say something . . . But no. He didn't want to any more. He just laughed it off. He felt himself being put into his overcoat, and his hat being rammed down over his eyes. He became aware of the cold dark landing and the stairs. Finally he tripped, and seemed to be falling into an abyss. He tried to cry out, and all of a sudden found he was in the courtyard. A chill blast of air struck him, and he stopped. Just at that moment he caught the sound of the orchestra striking up again. It all came back to him. His energy seemed suddenly restored. He had been standing rooted to the spot, but now he broke away, and rushed headlong out of the courtyard into the open, to freedom and wherever his legs might carry him.

## 5

Every tower in St. Petersburg that was wont
to tell and strike the hour sounded midnight
as Mr. Golyadkin rushed out, demented, onto
the Fontanka Embankment near the Izmaylovsky
Bridge, seeking safety from enemies and persecu-
tion, a shower of insults, the alarmed shrieks ot
the old ladies, the sobbing and sighing of the
other women, and the murderous glances ot
Andrey Filippovich. He had no more life in him.
He was finished in the full sense of the word, and
if at that moment he was still able to run, it was
only by some incredible miracle.

It was a dreadful night, a real November night,
dank, misty, rainy and snowy, a night pregnant
with colds, agues, quinsies, gumboils, and fevers
of every conceivable shape and size—put in a
nutshell, a night bestowing all the bounties of a
St. Petersburg November. The wind howled
through the streets, lashing the black waters of
the Fontanka high above the mooring rings, and
vigorously rattling the feeble lanterns along the
embankment, which responded with those thin,
ear-piercing squeaks, that compose the unceas-
ing concert of jarring sound so familiar to every
inhabitant of St. Petersburg. It was raining and

snowing all in one. The sheeting rain was broken up by the wind and sprayed almost horizontally, as if from a fireman's hose, stabbing and stinging the face of the unhappy Mr. Golyadkin like so many pins and needles. In the night stillness, disturbed only by the distant rumble of carriages, the howl of the wind and the squeak of the lanterns, was heard the dismal sound of water gushing and gurgling from every roof, porch, gutter and cornice, onto the granite pavement. There was not a soul anywhere, nor could there be it seemed, at such an hour in such weather. And so, alone with his despair, Mr. Golyadkin jogged along the Fontanka, taking his usual short quick steps, and hastening to reach as soon as possible his Shestilavochnaya Street, his fourth floor and his own rooms.

Although snow, rain and all the nameless afflictions of a wet and windy St. Petersburg November night were suddenly and with one accord assailing Mr. Golyadkin—weighed down as he was with enough misfortune already— giving no quarter or respite, gumming up his eyes, cutting into him from all sides, chilling him to the bone, and driving him off his path and out of his mind; although all this had fallen upon him at once as if by express agreement with his enemies to give him a day and a night he would not forget in a hurry, Mr. Golyadkin remained almost unaware of this final evidence of

a persecuting fate, so stunned and shaken was he
by all that had befallen him a few minutes earlier
at Civil Counsellor Berendeyev's. Any detached
and impartial observer who at that moment merely
glanced at Mr. Golyadkin and saw his anguished
step, would immediately have been imbued with
a sense of the appalling horror of his misfortunes,
and would certainly have said he had the look of
a man wishing to hide and escape from himself.
And that is exactly how it was. We will say more:
at that moment Mr. Golyadkin wanted not only
to escape from himself, but to annihilate himself
completely, to return to dust and cease to be. He
was oblivious of all around, and looked as if the
vexations of that vile night—the long walk, the
wind and the rain—no longer existed for him.
A galosh parting company with Mr. Golyadkin's
right boot, remained where it was in the slush
and snow of the Fontanka pavement. Mr. Golyadkin had no thought of going back for it, for he
had not noticed its loss. So great was his perplexity that every now and then, regardless of
everything around, he would stop short and stand
stock-still in the middle of the pavement, completely absorbed by the awfulness of his downfall.
At such moments he would depart this life and
cease to exist. Then suddenly, off he would go
like a madman, and run and run without looking
back, as though being pursued and fleeing some
still more dreadful calamity. His was indeed an

awful predicament. At last, his strength exhausted, Mr. Golyadkin stopped, and leaning over the railings like someone with a sudden nose-bleed, stared fixedly at the troubled black waters of the Fontanka. How long he spent thus engaged it is impossible to say. All one can say is that Mr. Golyadkin had then reached such depths of despair, had been so wearied, tormented and dispirited, that he had forgotten everything—the Izmaylovsky Bridge, Shestilavochnaya Street, and the position he was in. What did it matter? He didn't care. The thing was over and done with—signed, sealed and delivered. Why should he worry? . . . Suddenly he shuddered all over and instinctively leapt sideways a couple of yards. Filled with unspeakable uneasiness, he peered about him. But there was no one. Nothing out of the ordinary had happened, and yet . . . And yet he thought someone had just been standing right there beside him, also with elbows on the railings, and, strange to relate, had even spoken to him—had spoken quickly, jerkily and not altogether intelligibly, but had said something of intimate concern to him.

'Did I dream it?' said Mr. Golyadkin, again peering around. 'But where am I? Ugh!' he concluded, shaking his head, and began uneasily and fearfully to stare into the wet murky distance, straining his short-sighted eyes to the uttermost in an effort to penetrate the sodden darkness that lay before him. But there was nothing new.

Nothing peculiar struck Mr. Golyadkin's eye. Everything seemed to be as it should—the snow falling harder and thicker, not a thing visible over twenty yards, the lanterns squeaking even more shrilly than before, and the wind taking up its mournful song on an even more piteous and plaintive note, like an importunate beggar pleading for a copper for food.

'What's wrong with me?' thought Mr. Golyadkin, setting off on his way again, and still looking round occasionally. He felt a strange new sensation coming over him—a mixture of fear and anguish. . . . A feverish shudder ran through every nerve. It was an unbearably dreadful moment.

'Well, it doesn't matter,' he said to cheer himself up. 'Perhaps it's nothing, and not a disgrace to anyone's honour. Perhaps it had to be so,' he continued, not understanding himself what he was saying. 'Perhaps in due course this will all turn out for the best. There won't be anything to complain of, and everyone will be vindicated.'

So saying, and putting his mind at ease with words, Mr. Golyadkin shook himself off a bit and dislodged the snow with which his hat, collar, overcoat, scarf and boots were thickly encrusted. But he was still unable to shake off and rid himself of that strange vague feeling of anguish. Somewhere in the distance a cannon was fired.

'Fine weather this is,' thought our hero. 'Hark!

Won't that be for a flood? You can see the water's up too high.'

No sooner had Mr. Golyadkin said or thougth this than he saw someone coming towards him—someone who probably like himself had been delayed on some matter or other. A meaningless, quite fortuitous thing it seemed, but for some unknown reason Mr. Golyadkin was disturbed, scared even, and rather unsure of himself. Not that he was afraid of it being anyone unpleasant, but . . .

'Who knows who this belated fellow may be?' flashed through Mr. Golyadkin's mind. 'Perhaps he's the same as the rest . . . Perhaps *he's* the most important part of it, and isn't just out for his health but with the express purpose of crossing my path and provoking me.'

But Mr. Golyadkin may not exactly have thought this; he may momentarily have sensed something very disagreeable that was much the same. Still, there was no time for thoughts or sensations. The man was a couple of yards away. Mr. Golyadkin lost no time in assuming as was his wont a very special expression that said clearly that he, Golyadkin, was going his own way and was all right, that the road was wide enough for everyone, and that he, Golyadkin, was obviously doing no harm to anybody. Suddenly, as though struck by a thunderbolt, he stopped dead in his tracks, and spun round like a weathercock in the

wind to stare after the man who had passed and
was disappearing rapidly into the whirl of snow.
He also was in a hurry. He was dressed and
muffled exactly like Mr. Golyadkin from head to
foot, and was scuttling along the Fontanka at
almost a run, with the same short rapid step.

'What's this?' whispered Mr. Golyadkin—
there was a smile of incredulity on his face, but
his whole body was trembling. A cold shiver
ran down his spine. The man had meanwhile
disappeared completely, and the sound of his
footsteps could no longer be heard. But Mr.
Golyadkin still stood gazing after him. Gradually he recovered his senses.

'What is it?' he thought irritably. 'Have I
gone mad or something?'

He turned and went his way, walking steadily
faster and doing his best not to think. With this
object he even closed his eyes. Suddenly above
the howling wind and the noise of the storm he
again heard footsteps very close. He shuddered
and opened his eyes. Twenty yards away was
again the dark figure of a man drawing rapidly
nearer. He was hustling along at a brisk trot,
and the distance between them was diminishing
rapidly. Mr. Golyadkin could now see his new
late-night companion quite distinctly, and uttered
a cry of horror and amazement. His legs buckled
beneath him. It was the same man he had passed
ten minutes before! This and something else so

astounded Mr. Golyadkin that he stopped, gave
a cry, tried to say something, then rushed to over-
take the stranger, shouting in an attempt to halt
him as quickly as possible. The stranger halted
some ten yards from Mr. Golyadkin, where his
whole figure was illuminated by a nearby
lantern. He turned, and looking puzzled and
impatient, waited for what Mr. Golyadkin had
to say.

'Excuse me. Perhaps I'm mistaken,' quavered
our hero.

The stranger turned away with a gesture of
annoyance, and walked quickly on without a
word, as if in a hurry to make up the two seconds
wasted over Mr. Golyadkin. As for the latter, he
was trembling all over. His knees turned to jelly,
and with a groan he sat down on a tall kerbstone.
There was indeed cause for alarm, for he thought
there was something familiar about the stranger.
This by itself would have been nothing. But he
was now almost sure it was someone he knew.
He'd seen him often. He'd seen him somewhere
quite recently even. But where? Was it yesterday? But the fact that he'd seen him often wasn't
of primary importance, there was nothing very
special about him, nothing certainly that would
have made anyone look twice at him. He was
just like anyone else, of course, respectable, and
perhaps even had certain quite good points; he
was, in short, a man going his own way. Mr.

Golyadkin felt no hatred, enmity or even the slightest unfriendliness towards him—quite the reverse it would seem. And yet—and this was the main thing—he would not have wished to meet him for all the tea in China, and particularly under circumstances such as the present. Mr. Golyadkin, we must add, knew this man perfectly well, knew his name even. But again, not for all the tea in China would he have spoken his name, or been willing to admit that that over there was so-and-so whose father was so-and-so. How long Mr. Golyadkin's mental confusion lasted, or how long he remained seated on the kerbstone, we cannot say. But at last recovering somewhat, he took to his heels and ran as hard as he could without looking back. His lungs felt as if they would burst. Twice he tripped and nearly fell, and on one of these occasions his other boot parted company with its galosh. Finally he slackened his pace a little to get breath. A rapid glance round showed that he had without noticing it run the whole of his usual route along the Fontanka, crossed the Anichkov Bridge, and was now at the corner of Liteynaya Street, some way along the Nevsky Prospect. He turned into Liteynaya Street. At that moment he was in the position of a man standing on the brink of a fearful precipice when the ground gives way beneath him . . . A tremor—the ground moves, a last shudder—and it's falling with him into the abyss . . . The

hapless man has neither the strength nor the will-
power to leap back or to take his eyes from the
yawning chasm . . . He is drawn towards it,
and finally jumps to hasten his end. Mr. Golyadkin knew, felt and was quite convinced, that some
new evil would befall him on the way, and that
some fresh unpleasantness would burst upon him;
that there would be, for instance, another meeting
with the stranger. Oddly enough he even wanted
this to happen, considering it inevitable and only
asking that the whole thing might be got over as
quickly as possible, and that he might know where
he stood. Only let it be soon! Meanwhile he ran
on and on as though propelled by some external
force, for he felt numb and weak all over. He
was incapable of thought, but his mind clutched
brier-like at everything. A miserable little stray
dog, wet and shivering with cold, attached itself
to Mr. Golyadkin and trotted along beside him,
ears down and tail between its legs, every now and
then looking up at him, timidly and intelligently.
A long-forgotten idea, a recollection of something
that had happened in the distant past now came
into his head and hammered away there, irritating
him and refusing to let him be.

'Ugh! Wretched little dog!' muttered Mr.
Golyadkin, not understanding what he was saying.

At last he caught sight of his stranger at the
corner of Italyanskaya Street. But now instead
of coming towards him, he was going in the same

direction. He was several yards in front, and also running. They turned into Shestilavochnaya Street. Mr. Golyadkin caught his breath. The stranger had stopped right outside the house in which he lived. The bell rang, and the iron bolt grated back almost simultaneously. The wicket opened, the stranger stooped, remained visible for a second, then disappeared. Mr. Golyadkin got there at almost the same moment, and went through the wicket like a shot out of a gun. Ignoring the grumbling porter, he rushed breathlessly into the courtyard and for a moment regained sight of his interesting companion at the foot of the staircase leading to his rooms. He hurled himself in pursuit. The staircase was dark dank and dirty, and mountains of junk belonging to tenants blocked every landing. Any stranger journeying up it after dark would run the risk of breaking a leg, and would be forced to spend about half an hour over it, cursing the staircase together with his friends for having settled in such a place. But Mr. Golyadkin's companion was darting lightly up the stairs, encountering no difficulties, and showing perfect knowledge of the ground. Mr. Golyadkin nearly caught him up. Several times the hem of the stranger's coat brushed his nose. Suddenly his heart sank. The mysterious man had stopped and knocked at the door of Mr. Golyadkin's flat. Petrushka answered at once as if he had been waiting up (at any other time this would have surprised Mr. Golyadkin), and lighted the stranger in with a candle. Half out of his wits our hero followed, and without removing hat or overcoat, dashed down the short corridor. On the threshold of his room he stopped as though struck by a thunderbolt. His worst fears were realised . . . Everything he had dreaded and foreseen was now fact. Sitting on *his* bed, also wearing a hat and coat, smiling slightly, puckering up his eyes and tipping him a friendly nod, was the stranger. Mr. Golyadkin wanted to scream, but could not—wanted to make some form of protest, but lacked the power. His hair stood on end, and he collapsed senseless with horror on the spot. And small wonder. He had fully recognized his friend of the night. It was none other than himself—Mr. Golyadkin . . . Another Mr. Golyadkin, but exactly the same as him . . . It was, in short, his double . . .

## 6

Next morning at eight precisely, Mr. Golyadkin came to, lying in bed. Immediately he
remembered and saw in his mind's eye the full
horror of all the extraordinary events of the preceding day, and the almost impossible adventures
of the whole incredibly strange night. Such fierce
diabolical malice on the part of his enemies, particularly as last demonstrated, made Mr. Golyadkin's
blood run cold. But at the same time it was all
so peculiar, incomprehensible and absurd, it all
seemed so impossible even, that really one could
hardly credit it. Mr. Golyadkin would have been
only too ready to regard the whole thing as a
delirious fancy, a momentary derangement of the
imagination or a clouding of the mind, had he not
fortunately known from bitter experience of life
the lengths to which a man may sometimes be
driven by malice, and the furious extremes to
which an enemy avenging pride and honour may
sometimes go. The reality of last night's walk and
to some extent of what had occurred during that
walk, was, moreover, confirmed and supported
by his weary limbs, his muzzy head, his breaking
back and hacking cough. And finally he had
known for ages that they were cooking something

up, and that there was someone else in with them.
But what of it? On mature consideration Mr.
Golyadkin decided to keep quiet, to yield, and not
protest until a certain time.

'Perhaps their idea was just to give me a fright,
and when they see me not minding or protesting,
but submitting and humbly putting up with it,
they'll give way first.'

Such were the thoughts that ran through the
mind of Mr. Golyadkin, as, stretching himself in
bed and easing his aching limbs, he lay waiting
for Petrushka to make his usual appearance. He
had already been waiting for about a quarter of
an hour, listening to the lazy fellow fussing about
with the samovar behind the partition, but unable
to make up his mind to call him. One might go
further and say that Mr. Golyadkin was a little
scared of facing Petrushka.

'Heaven knows what he thinks about it all, the
scoundrel,' he thought. 'Doesn't say a word, but
he's crafty.'

At last the door creaked and Petrushka appeared,
bearing a tray. Mr. Golyadkin watched him
timidly out of the corner of his eye, waiting impatiently for something to happen, waiting to see
whether he'd say anything on a certain matter.
Petrushka said not a word, and was somehow even
more sullen and uncommunicative than usual. He
squinted darkly around, and was quite clearly extremely displeased about something. He did not

so much as glance at his master, and this we may observe somewhat irritated the latter. He put everything he had brought on the table, turned, and disappeared behind his partition without a word.

'He knows! He knows all about it, the good-for-nothing!' muttered Mr. Golyadkin as he set to to drink his tea. But although Petrushka came in several times for various things, he put no questions to him.

Mr. Golyadkin was most agitated. The thought of going to the office terrified him. He had a strong presentiment of something being not quite right there.

'If you go, you'll run slap into it,' he thought. 'Isn't the best thing now to be patient for a bit? Wouldn't it be better to wait, and let them get on as they like? I could wait here today, getting my strength back, recuperating and thinking it all out. Then I could pick a moment, and give them the surprise of their lives, and pretend nothing whatever was wrong.'

Pondering thus, Mr. Golyadkin smoked one pipe after another. Time flew, and soon it was almost half past nine.

'Well, it's half past nine,' thought Mr. Golyadkin. 'It's late to go now. Apart from that I'm ill. Of course I'm ill. Who's to say I'm not? And if they send anyone to see—let the administrative officer come if he likes—what do I care?

I've got backache. I've got a cough. I've got a
cold in the head, and I can't go. I can't possibly
in this weather. I might be taken ill, and die.
There's a heavy death-rate nowadays . . .'

At last, by means of such arguments, Mr.
Golyadkin salved his conscience completely, and
justified himself in advance against the reprimand
he might expect from Andrey Filippovich for
neglecting his work. In all such situations our
hero was very fond of justifying himself in his own
eyes by various irrefutable arguments, and so
salving his conscience completely. And so, his
conscience salved, he picked up his pipe, filled it,
and had no sooner got it drawing nicely, than he
sprang up from the sofa, tossed it away, quickly
washed, shaved and combed his hair, dragged on
his uniform jacket and other things, and grabbing
some papers, shot off to the office.

Timidly Mr. Golyadkin entered his section,
trembling in anticipation of something extremely
nasty, trembling with an expectancy which, if
unconscious and vague, was at the same time
unpleasant. Timidly he seated himself at his
usual place next to Anton Antonovich Setochkin,
the chief clerk. Without looking round or allowing himself to be distracted, he buried himself in
the papers before him. He had decided and promised himself to keep as far aloof as possible
from anything provocative, anything that could
in any way compromise him, such as indelicate

questions, unseemly insinuations, and pleasantries
about the events of the preceding night; he had
even made up his mind to forgo the usual cour-
tesies with his colleagues—inquiries as to their
health etc. But to keep this up was obviously an
impossibility. Uneasiness and uncertainty about
something that touched him intimately always
tormented him more than the thing itself. And
that is why, despite his promise not to become
involved whatever happened, and to keep aloof
from everything, no matter what it was, Mr.
Golyadkin kept raising his head, furtively and
ever so slightly, to take a sly peep at the faces of
his colleagues to left and right, in an attempt to
decide whether anything new or special concerning him was for some improper reason being concealed. He supposed there to be a direct connexion
between everything at that moment around him
and what had happened the day before. At last
he began to wish in his anguish that it might
all end as speedily as possible, though heaven
alone knew how—in some disaster if need be—
it didn't matter! Fate took him at his word. No
sooner had he made the wish, than his doubts
were resolved, albeit in a most peculiar and unexpected manner.

The door of the next room opened with a timid
little squeak as if to announce a person of no great
consequence, and a figure, well known to Mr.
Golyadkin, came and stood diffidently before the

desk at which he was sitting. Our hero did not
raise his head. No. One fleeting glance at this
figure, and he knew, he understood it all to the
last detail. He flushed with shame, and just as
the ostrich pursued by a hunter hides its head in
the burning sand, so Mr. Golyadkin buried his
wretched head in his papers. The newcomer
bowed to Andrey Filippovich, and then could be
heard those silkily formal tones in which the heads
of all government departments are wont to
address newly-arrived subordinates.

'Sit here,' said Andrey Filippovich, indicating
Anton Antonovich's desk to the new recruit. 'Sit
here opposite Mr. Golyadkin, and we'll give you
some work right away.' He ended with a rapid
and decorous admonitory wave of the hand, and
was lost in the perusal of various documents from
the great pile in front of him.

At last Mr. Golyadkin raised his eyes, and if he
did not faint away, it was solely because he had
had from the first a presentiment of the whole
thing, had been forewarned, and had already
known in his heart who the newcomer was. His
first move was to take a rapid glance around to
see whether there was any whispering, whether
any office witticisms were taking shape on the
subject, whether anyone's face expressed surprise,
and finally whether anyone had collapsed beneath
his desk with fright. But to his great astonishment
he could detect nothing of the sort. He was

amazed by his friends' and colleagues' behaviour.
It seemed beyond the bounds of common sense.
He was even frightened by such unusual silence.
The reality of the thing spoke for itself. It was
strange, hideous, absurd. It *was* something to
make a stir about. All this of course, merely
flashed through Mr. Golyadkin's mind. He felt as
if he was being slowly roasted alive, and not
without reason. Sitting opposite, was the terror
of Mr. Golyadkin, the shame of Mr. Golyadkin,
his nightmare of the day before, in short, Mr.
Golyadkin himself; not the one who was now
sitting on his chair with mouth agape and a dry
pen in his hand; not the one who was assistant
to the chief clerk; not the one who liked to efface
and hide himself in the crowd; not the one who
said plainly by the way he walked, 'Don't touch
me, and I won't touch you,' or 'Don't touch me,
I'm not hurting you.' No. This was a different
Mr. Golyadkin, quite different but at the same
time identical with the first—the same height,
same build, dressed the same, bald in the same
place; in short, the resemblance was perfect;
nothing, absolutely nothing had been omitted, so
that had they been stood side by side, not a soul
would have undertaken to say who was the real
Mr. Golyadkin, and who the counterfeit, who the
old, and who the new, who the original and who
the copy.

Our hero, if comparison is possible, was like a

man on whom some wag has secretly focussed a burning-glass by way of a joke.

'Is it a dream, or isn't it?' wondered Mr. Golyadkin. 'Is it real, or is it yesterday's business continued? But how can it? What right has this to happen? Who admitted this clerk? Who authorized it? Am I asleep? Am I dreaming?'

Mr. Golyadkin tried pinching himself, and even thought of pinching somebody else . . . No, it wasn't a dream, so that was that. He felt the sweat pouring from him. What was happening to him was, he sensed, unprecedented, unheard-of, and therefore, to crown his misfortune, unseemly, for he perceived and understood the full disadvantage of being the first example of such lampoonery. He began finally even to doubt his own existence, and although he had been prepared for everything in advance, and had himself wished for his doubts to be resolved in some way, what had happened was, of course, in the nature of a surprise. He was wrung with anguish. Now and then he would lose all power of reasoning and lapse into unconsciousness. After one such moment he recovered to find himself automatically and unconsciously guiding his pen over the paper. Not trusting himself, he began checking what he had written, but could make nothing of it.

At last, the other Mr. Golyadkin, who all this while had been sitting quietly and decorously at his place, got up, and disappeared into the other section on some matter. Mr. Golyadkin took a look around, but there was nothing. All was still. Nothing could be heard but the scratching of pens, the rustle of turning pages, and a murmur of conversation from corners a little further removed from the seat of Andrey Filippovich. Mr. Golyadkin glanced at Anton Antonovich, and seeing our hero's expression, which in all likelihood reflected his mood at that moment, and was in keeping with the whole drift of the affair, the good Anton Antonovich laid aside his pen, and with unusual concern inquired after Mr. Golyadkin's health.

'I-I-I'm all right, Anton Antonovich. I'm perfectly well, Anton Antonovich,' stammered Mr. Golyadkin. 'I've nothing at the moment to complain of, Anton Antonovich,' he added uncertainly, not yet fully trusting this Anton Antonovich whose name he was using so freely.

'There. I thought you were poorly. It wouldn't have been surprising, I'm afraid. All sorts of epidemics about, especially at present, you know.'

'Yes, Anton Antonovich, I know there are . . . But Anton Antonovich, that's not the reason for which I . . .' continued Mr. Golyadkin, staring hard at him. 'You see, Anton Antonovich—I don't know how to put it to you—that is, I mean, from what angle to tackle this matter . . .'

'What was that? I confess I don't quite follow

you, you know. You . . . um . . . You tell me a
bit more fully what the trouble is,' said Anton
Antonovich who, seeing the tears start to Mr.
Golyadkin's eyes, was becoming a little troubled
himself.

'I really . . . There's a clerk here, Anton
Antonovich . . .'

'Well? I still don't follow.'

'What I mean, Anton Antonovich, is that there's
a newly-arrived clerk here.'

'Yes. A namesake of yours.'

'Wh-a-t?' cried Mr. Golyadkin.

'A namesake of yours. He's Golyadkin, too.
Your brother, perhaps?'

'No, Anton Antonovich, I . . .'

'Hm. You don't say. I thought he must be a
near relation. There's a certain family resemblance,
you know.'

Mr. Golyadkin was stunned with amazement,
and for a while, speechless. How *could* he treat
so lightly a thing so unparalleled and monstrous
—a thing so rare in its way as to astound the most
uninterested observer! How *could* anyone speak of
a family resemblance, when here was a mirror
image!

'Do you know what I advise you to do, Yakov
Petrovich?' continued Anton Antonovich—'go
and see a doctor and ask his advice. Somehow
you don't *look* at all well, you know. Your eyes
have got a funny look about them.'

'No, Anton Antonovich, naturally I feel . . .
That is, what sort of a person is he, this clerk?
That's what I want to know.'

'Yes?'

'That is, haven't you noticed something peculiar
about him, Anton Antonovich—something very
significant?'

'What exactly?'

'I mean a striking resemblance to someone—to
me for instance. Just now you said something,
just a casual remark, about a family resemblance . . .
Do you know twins are sometimes as alike
as two peas in a pod, so that you can't tell one
from the other? Well, that's what I'm talking
about . . .'

'Yes,' said Anton Antonovich, after pondering
for a moment, as though this had never struck him
before. 'Yes. Quite right. Really, the resemblance is amazing, and you're perfectly correct
—you could be taken for one another,' he continued, with a look of ever-increasing astonishment. 'Do you know, it's a wonderful—it's a
fantastic likeness, as they sometimes say. He's you
exactly . . . Have you noticed, Yakov Petrovich?
I meant to ask you about it myself. I must confess,
I wasn't paying proper attention at first. It's a
wonder, it really is! And tell me, Yakov Petrovich, you weren't born here, were you?'

'No.'

'Neither was he. Perhaps you're from the same

parts. Where did your mother spend most of her life, if you don't mind my asking?'

'Did you say . . . Did you say he wasn't born here, Anton Antonovich?'

'No, he's not from these parts. It's an absolute marvel,' continued the loquacious Anton Antonovich, for whom it was a real treat to have something to prattle about.

'It really does make you curious. The number of times you pass him, brush up against him or knock into him, and don't notice. But don't you worry. It's a thing that does happen. Do you know, I must tell you this, the very same thing occurred to an aunt of mine on my mother's side. She saw her own spit and image before she died . . .'

'No, I . . . Forgive my interrupting you, Anton Antonovich, but what I should like to know is how this clerk—that is, how does he stand here?'

'He's got the vacancy left by Semyon Ivanovich who died. A place fell vacant, so they put him in. A good-hearted fellow, poor Semyon Ivanovich. Left three little kiddies, so they say. His widow came, and went down on her knees to his Excellency. But they say she hides it away. She's got a bit of money, but she hides it . . .'

'No, I'm still on about the other thing, Anton Antonovich.'

'What's that? Ah, yes. But why are you so concerned about it? Don't worry, that's what I say. It'll all pass. What does it matter? It's no affair of yours. It's God's doing, it's His will, and to grumble at that is a sin. *His* infinite wisdom is apparent in this, and you, Yakov Petrovich, so far as I can gather, are in no way to blame. The world is full of wonders! Mother Nature is generous. And by way of example, while we're on the subject, you've heard, I take it, about—what d'you call 'em—the Siamese twins, being joined back to back, and living, eating and sleeping together like it. They earn good money, people say.'

'Anton Antonovich, allow me . . .'

'I take your meaning. Well, what of it? It doesn't matter. I tell you, to my mind there's nothing to get upset about. He's a clerk just like anyone else—seems a capable chap. Says he's called Golyadkin. Isn't from hereabouts, he says, and he's a clerk. He's had a personal talk with his Excellency.'

'What about?'

'Oh, nothing. Gave an adequate account of himself, they say. Stated his case: "Such and such, and such and such, your Excellency. I've no fortune, I'd like to serve, and would be especially proud to do so under you . . ." Well, everything as it should be, you know. Put it all very nicely. Must be a clever fellow. Came with a recommendation, of course. Can't do much without one, you know.'

'Who was it from? What I mean is, who exactly is mixed up in this scandalous business?'

'Oh, yes. It was a good recommendation, so they say. They say his Excellency had a laugh with Andrey Filippovich over it.'

'Had a laugh with Andrey Filippovich?'

'Yes. He just smiled, and said it was all right, and he had no objections, provided he did his job properly . . .'

'Well, what happened next? You're cheering me up quite a bit, Anton Antonovich. Tell me what happened next, I beg you.'

'Forgive me. Again I don't quite . . . Ah well, it's no matter. It's quite simple. Don't you go worrying, that's what I say. There's nothing fishy about it . . .'

'No, what I want to ask you, Anton Antonovich, is, didn't his Excellency add anything to that, about me for instance?'

'Oh, certainly! Or rather, no, not a thing. You can be quite easy in your mind. Do you know—it's striking enough, of course, yet at first . . . Well, take me for instance. I almost missed it at first. Why I didn't notice till you mentioned it, I don't know, I'm sure. But still, you can be easy in your mind. He said nothing special, nothing whatever,' added the good Anton Antonovich, rising from his seat.

'Well, Anton Antonovich, I . . .'

'Er, look, excuse me, will you? Here I've been, babbling away, and I've got something urgent and important to do. I must get it finished.'

'Anton Antonovich,' came a polite summons from Andrey Filippovich, 'his Excellency has been asking for you.'

'Coming, Andrey Filippovich, coming at once.'

And grabbing a pile of papers, Anton Antonovich sped first to Andrey Filippovich, and then into his Excellency's room.

'So that's how we stand,' thought Mr. Golyadkin to himself. 'So that's the way things are. Not bad. Things have taken a much pleasanter turn,' he said to himself, rubbing his hands, and in his joy, oblivious of everything.

'So it's quite ordinary, this business of ours. It's all come to nothing. It's all blowing over. No one's noticed in fact. Not a squeak out of them, the cut-throats—they're sitting and getting on with their work. Splendid! Splendid!

'I like the man, always have done, and respect him . . . But now I come to think of it, I'd be afraid to trust him with anything. He's very grey and doddery is Anton Antonovich. Still, the main and most important thing is his Excellency's not saying anything, but just letting it pass. That's good. I approve of that. Only why's Andrey Filippovich got to butt in with his sneers? What's it got to do with him? Crafty old devil! He's always in your way, always trying to mess things up, always crossing and spiting, spiting and crossing you!'

Mr. Golyadkin took another look round, and was again encouraged. But a vague and unpleasant idea that he had, nevertheless troubled him. The thought crossed his mind of somehow enlisting the support of the clerks, of somehow stealing a march on them, and, approaching them ostensibly on business, or as they were all leaving, of making in the course of conversation some reference to the subject such as 'Such and such, and such and such, gentlemen—a striking resemblance—very strange—sailing under false colours, that's what it is.' Thus, by treating it as a joke, he would gauge the extent of the danger. For still waters ran deep, he concluded. But his thought remained nothing more than a thought. He changed his mind in time. He realized that would be going too far.

'That's you all over!' he said, tapping his forehead. 'Now you'll be full of fun. You're happy! Honest soul that you are. No. We'd better have patience, Yakov Petrovich. We'll have patience and wait.'

None the less Mr. Golyadkin was, as we have mentioned, filled with renewed hope, and felt like someone risen from the dead.

'It's all right,' he thought. 'It's like having a ton-weight off your chest. "To open it you

simply raised the lid."* It's as simple as that.
Krylov's right. He knows all about it. He's an
artful one, Krylov, and a great fable-writer!

'And as far as this other fellow is concerned, let
him work here. Let him, and good luck to him,
provided he doesn't hinder or interfere with anyone. Let him—he's got my consent and approval!'

All this time the hours had been slipping by,
and four struck before Mr. Golyadkin noticed it.
Office hours were over. Andrey Filippovich went
for his hat, and as usual everyone followed his
example. Mr. Golyadkin hung about for a bit,
deliberately leaving last, after everyone had gone
their separate ways. Once out in the street, he
felt as if he was in paradise, so much so that he
conceived a desire to make a detour and go along
the Nevsky Prospect.

'It's fate—everything taking this unexpected
turn,' said our hero. 'And the weather's better.
There's a nice frost, and sledges are out. Frost's
good for a Russian. I like Russians. And there's
a bit of snow—*fresh-fallen* snow as a hunter would
say. That's the time to go after hares, when there's
fresh-fallen snow. Ah well! It doesn't matter.'

Thus did Mr. Golyadkin express his delight,
but all the while there was a sort of anxiety at the

* Last line of a fable by I. A. Krylov describing the clever
attempts made to open a certain box in every way but the obvious,
and suggesting that difficulties should not be seen where they
do not exist.—*Translator*.

back of his mind, and at times a gnawing pain at
his heart for which he could find no relief.

'Still, we'll wait a day before we start rejoicing.
But what's wrong? We'll think it all out, and
see. Well, come on my young friend, let's think
it out then. First of all, there's someone like you,
exactly like you. Well, what is there in that?
Supposing there is—any need for me to cry over
it? What's it matter to me? I'm out of it all. I
don't care, and that's that. I accept it, and there
you are. Let him work in the office! It's strange
and wonderful, they say, about the Siamese
twins ... Well, why drag them in? Suppose they
are twins—even great men have looked silly at
times. History even tells us the great Suvorov
used to crow like a cock ... Still, all that was for
political reasons. And even the great generals ...
But what are generals? I go my own way. I
don't bother about anyone else, and being innocent, I scorn my enemies. I'm no intriguer, and
proud of the fact. Frank, upright, mild, agreeable, orderly ...'

Mr. Golyadkin broke off suddenly, began
trembling like a leaf, and shut his eyes for a moment. Trusting what had frightened him to have
been an illusion, however, he opened them again,
and glanced timidly to the right out of the corner
of his eye. It was no illusion! Trotting along
beside him, smiling, looking straight at him, and
waiting, it seemed, for a chance to start a con-

versation, was the person whose acquaintance he had made that morning. But conversation was not started. They continued thus for about fifty yards. All Mr. Golyadkin's efforts were directed towards muffling himself up as much as possible, burying himself in his overcoat, and pulling his hat as far as it would go down over his eyes. To add insult to injury, even the other's hat and coat were identical with Mr. Golyadkin's—they might have been taken from his own back.

'We go different ways, it seems, sir . . .' said Mr. Golyadkin finally, not looking at his friend and trying to keep his voice to a whisper. 'I'm quite sure we do,' he said after a short pause. 'I'm sure you at last take my meaning,' he threw in rather stiffly.

'I should like . . .' said Mr. Golyadkin's friend at last. 'I should like . . . You'll kindly forgive me, I hope . . . I don't know who to turn to here . . . Placed as I am . . . I trust you'll excuse my making so bold, but I thought you were so sympathetic as to take some interest in me this morning. Speaking for myself, I felt drawn to you from the first. I . . .'

At this point Mr. Golyadkin silently wished that his new colleague might disappear through the ground.

'If I might venture to hope that you would condescend to hear me out, Yakov Petrovich . . .'

'Here we're, er . . . We'd better go to my

place,' replied Mr. Golyadkin. 'Let's cross the Nevsky now. It's more convenient for us on the other side. Then there's a little side street we can take . . . Yes, we'd better do that.'

'Yes, certainly, we'll take the little side street,' said Mr. Golyadkin's submissive companion, seeming to intimate by his diffident tone that he could not pick and choose, and that, situated as he was, he was prepared to be satisfied with the little side street.

As for Mr. Golyadkin, he had no idea what was happening to him. He could not trust his own senses. He had not yet recovered from his astonishment.

## 7

O N the stairs and at the door of his rooms he recovered a little.

'What a dim-wit I am!' he chided himself. 'Where am I taking him? I'm putting a rope around my own neck. What will Petrushka think, seeing us together? What won't the wretch think now! He's suspicious as it is . . .'

But it was too late for any regrets. Mr. Golyadkin knocked, the door opened and Petrushka began helping guest and master out of their coats. Mr. Golyadkin stole a quick look, just a glance at Petrushka, in an attempt to read his thoughts from his face. But to his great astonishment his servant showed no surprise—quite the reverse, as if he had been expecting something of the sort. Of course, he was far from friendly. He wouldn't look you in the eye, and seemed all set to bite someone's head off.

'What's wrong today? Is everyone under a spell?' thought our hero. 'Some demon must have been around. Certainly something has got into them. What a damned worry it is!'

Such were Mr. Golyadkin's reflections as he conducted his guest into his room, and humbly invited him to take a seat. The guest showed every sign of being acutely embarrassed and overcome

with shyness, dutifully watched his host's every
move and caught his every glance, striving, it
seemed, to divine what he was thinking. There
was something abject, downtrodden and fearful
about every gesture he made, so that at this
moment he was, if one may use the simile, rather
like a man who, having no clothes of his own,
has donned someone else's, and can feel the sleeves
riding up and the waist nearly round the back or
his neck, and is all the time pulling down the
miserably short waistcoat; he edges away, tries
hard to hide, looks at every face to see if people
are ashamed on his account or laughing at him,
strains his ears to find out if they're discussing his
affairs; he goes red, and gets confused; his pride
suffers. Mr. Golyadkin had put his hat on the
window ledge. A sudden careless movement
knocked it to the floor. At once his guest shot
forward, picked it up, dusted it off, and carefully
replaced it, putting his own on the floor beside a
chair on the very edge of which he meekly perched
himself. This trivial incident was something of an
eye-opener to Mr. Golyadkin. Realizing that his
guest was in sore straits, he no longer felt at a loss
how to begin, but very properly left it all to him.
But he would not begin either, and waited for his
host to make the opening—whether this was out
of shyness, embarrassment or politeness, would be
difficult to say. At this moment Petrushka appeared, and stood in the doorway, his eyes fixed

on the opposite corner of the room to that in which his master and the guest were sitting.

'Shall I bring dinner for two?' he asked casually, in his rather husky voice.

'I—I don't know . . . Er, yes—dinner for two.'

Mr. Golyadkin glanced at his guest, and saw that he had gone as red as a beetroot. Being a kind-hearted person, he formed a theory accordingly.

'Poor fellow,' he thought, 'only been at the office a day. Probably been through it in his time. Only got what he stands up in, perhaps, and can't afford dinner. What a downtrodden specimen he is! Well, it doesn't matter. It's better like that in some ways . . .'

'Forgive my asking,' began Mr. Golyadkin, 'but what are your Christian names?'

'I'm—I'm Yakov Petrovich,' said the guest almost in a whisper, as though ashamed, embarrassed and apologetic that this should be so.

'Yakov Petrovich!' echoed our hero, unable to hide his confusion.

'Yes, that's right. . . . We're namesakes,' replied Mr. Golyadkin's lowly visitor, making so bold as to smile and say something jocular. But seeing his host was in no mood for jocularity, he immediately stopped short and assumed a most serious but rather embarrassed look.

'Er . . . May I ask to what I can attribute the honour . . .?'

'Knowing you to be upright and generous,' interposed his guest quickly but timidly, half rising from his seat, 'I have ventured to appeal to you for your friendship and protection,' he concluded, finding obvious difficulty in expressing himself, and selecting words that were not too adulatory and not too self-abasing, to avoid hurting his pride, nor yet too bold and savouring of an equality that was not proper. Mr. Golyadkin's guest was, as one might put it, behaving like a beggar of gentle birth who, with darns in his coat and the papers appropriate to his true status in his pocket, has not yet learnt how to stretch out his palm.

'You embarrass me,' replied Mr. Golyadkin, looking down at himself, at the walls of his room, and then at his guest. 'How can I . . . what I mean is, in what respect can I be of service to you?'

'I felt drawn to you at first sight, Yakov Petrovich, and—be so generous as to forgive me—I dared to put my trust in you. I . . . I'm all at sea here, Yakov Petrovich. I'm poor. I've suffered much, Yakov Petrovich, and I'm still new here. Discovering that you, with all the innate good qualities of a noble spirit, were of the same name as myself . . .'

Mr. Golyadkin frowned.

'. . . And were from the same parts, I resolved to come and acquaint you with my difficult position.'

'Quite so, quite so. I don't know what to say, I'm sure,' replied Mr. Golyadkin disconcertedly. 'Look, we'll have a talk after dinner.'

The guest bowed. Dinner was brought in. Petrushka placed everything on the table, and guest and host set about satisfying their appetites. The meal did not last long for both ate hurriedly—the host because he was not his usual self and felt ashamed that the dinner was bad when he would have liked to do his guest well, and show that he did not live like a pauper—the guest because he was extremely shy and embarrassed. Having once helped himself to a slice of bread and eaten it, he was afraid to reach out a second time. He scrupulously avoided taking the best of anything, and every minute assured his host that he wasn't hungry, that the meal was excellent, and that he was completely satisfied and would remember it till the day he died. The meal over, Mr. Golyadkin lit his pipe, and offered another that he had acquired for friends, to his guest. They seated themselves facing each other, and the guest began his tale.

The tale of Golyadkin junior lasted three or four hours, and was composed of the most trivial, one might almost say the most footling, incidents. It spoke of service in some provincial law-courts, of presidents and prosecutors, of office intrigues, of the rottenness of one of the chief clerks, of an inspector, of a sudden change of departmental head, and of how Golyadkin II had suffered entirely through no fault of his own; it spoke of his aged aunt Pelageya Semyonova, of how through the various machinations of his enemies he had lost his post and walked to St. Petersburg; it spoke of his wretched and painful existence in that city, of his long, fruitless search for a job, of how he exhausted his funds, spent his last penny on food, practically lived in the street, ate stale bread moistened by his own tears, and slept on bare boards; it spoke finally of how some kind person had taken trouble on his behalf, had given him introductions and magnanimously found him a new position. In the telling of this Mr. Golyadkin's guest wept and dabbed away his tears with a blue check handkerchief that looked very much like a piece of oilcloth. In conclusion he opened his heart to Mr. Golyadkin, and confessed that he was for the moment not only without means to support himself and settle in somewhere, but also quite unable to fit himself out properly. He had not even been able to raise the price of an old pair of boots, and his uniform he had borrowed for a short while.

Mr. Golyadkin was moved, was genuinely touched. Trivial as his guest's story had been, he had received every word of it like manna from heaven. Forgetting his recent misgivings, he allowed himself to feel joyously free, and mentally wrote himself down as a fool. It was all so natural!

What a thing to get distressed and alarmed about! Actually there *was* one thorny point, but it didn't matter. It couldn't disgrace you, damage your pride and ruin your career when you were innocent—when Nature herself was involved. Moreover the guest had begged his protection, had wept and accused fate; he seemed so simple, so completely without malice or artifice, so pathetic and insignificant; and now, although it might have been for other reasons, he too appeared embarrassed by the strange resemblance he bore to his host. His behaviour was completely dependable. His very expression was intended to please his host, and was that of a man tormented by pangs of conscience and a feeling of guilt. If, for instance, conversation touched on any doubtful point, the guest at once agreed with Mr. Golyadkin. If, by an oversight, he somehow advanced an opinion that was contrary to Mr. Golyadkin's, and then noticed his slip, he would immediately correct himself, explain, and give his host to understand that he thought exactly the same and viewed the whole thing in precisely the same light as he. In short, he did his level best to win Mr. Golyadkin over, and the latter finally decided he must be a most likable fellow in every way.

Tea was served. It was now after eight. Mr. Golyadkin felt in excellent spirits. He livened up, began to enjoy himself and get into his stride a bit, and finally launched out into a most lively and

entertaining conversation with his guest. Sometimes, in merry mood, Mr. Golyadkin was fond
of recounting odd items of interest. So it was now.
He told his guest a great deal about the capital, its
entertainments and its beauties; he told of the
theatre, the clubs and of Brülow's latest picture;
of the two Englishmen who travelled from
England to St. Petersburg expressly to see the
railings outside The Summer Gardens, and then
went straight home again; of his work at the
office, of Olsufy Ivanovich and Andrey Filippovich; he told how Russia was hourly approaching
perfection, and literature and learning were thriv-
ing; he told of an anecdote he had read lately in
*The Northern Bee*; he told of an extraordinarily
powerful boa constrictor in India; and lastly he
spoke of Baron Brambeus. In brief, Mr. Golyadkin was perfectly happy. His mind was completely
at ease; far from fearing his enemies, he was now
ready to challenge the lot of them to a decisive
battle; and he was acting as someone's protector,
and at last doing good. But in his heart of hearts
he confessed that he was still not quite happy, and
that even now another tiny little worry was
gnawing away inside him. He was much tormented by the memory of the previous evening at
Olsufy Ivanovich's. At that moment he would
have given a lot to wipe out some of the events of
the day before.

'Still, it doesn't matter,' decided our hero

finally, firmly resolving that he would henceforth behave himself, and not perpetrate such blunders.

Now that he had let himself go and was happy, Mr. Golyadkin had a mind to enjoy life a bit. Rum was brought in by Petrushka, and punch made. Guest and host drank one glass, then a second. The guest became more likable than ever, and more than once gave evidence of having a happy forthright nature. He entered wholeheartedly into Mr. Golyadkin's joyous mood, seemed to rejoice at his rejoicing, and to look upon him as his one true benefactor. Taking a pen and a small sheet of paper, he begged Mr. Golyadkin not to watch, and then when he had finished showed him what he had written. It was a quatrain, rather sentimental but elegantly phrased, beautifully penned, and evidently of the amiable guest's own composition. It ran thus:

> If me thou ever shouldst forget,
>   I'll remember thee;
> Much in life may happen yet,
>   But remember me!

With tears in his eyes, Mr. Golyadkin embraced his guest, and finally, overcome with emotion, let him into some of his secrets, with particular reference to Andrey Filippovich and Klara Olsufyevna.

'Yes Yakov Petrovich, we'll be friends, you and I,' said our hero. 'We were made for each other. We're like twin brothers. We'll fox 'em, my dear fellow. We'll fox 'em together. We'll start an intrigue of our own to spite them, that's what we'll do. Don't you trust any of them. I know you, and understand you, Yakov Petrovich. You're an honest soul. You'd go and tell them everything. You keep away from them all, my dear chap.'

The guest agreed to everything, thanked Mr. Golyadkin, and shed a few tears of his own.

'I tell you what, Yasha,' continued Mr. Golyadkin, his voice weak and quivering, 'you come and move in here for a time, or come for good. We'll get on all right. How does that appeal to you, eh? It's no good worrying or grumbling about this strange thing between us. It's a sin to grumble, my friend. It's Nature! And Mother Nature is generous, Yasha! I'm saying this because of my affection, my brotherly affection for you. We'll fox 'em, Yasha, you and I. We'll do some underhand work of our own, and make 'em laugh on the other side of their faces.'

They had had a third and a fourth glass of punch, and Mr. Golyadkin was becoming aware of two things: an extraordinary feeling of happiness, and an inability to stand. The guest was naturally invited to spend the night, and somehow a bed was made by placing together two rows of chairs.

Mr. Golyadkin junior declared that under a
friendly roof bare boards would make a soft couch,
and that he would sleep anywhere, humbly and
gratefully; he was now in Paradise; he had been
through a great deal in his time, had known
tears and sorrow, and had endured much; and
might, for who knew what the future held, have
more to endure. Mr. Golyadkin senior protested
at this, and began to argue that one should put full
trust in God. The guest entirely agreed, remarking that there was, of course, no one like God.
Mr. Golyadkin senior observed that the Turks were
in some respects right to invoke the name of God
even in sleep. Then, while disagreeing with the
aspersions cast by some scholars upon the Turkish
prophet Mohammed, and recognising him as a
great politician in his way, Mr. Golyadkin proceeded to an extremely interesting account of an
Algerian barber's shop that he had read in some
miscellany. Guest and host laughed heartily at the
artlessness of the Turks, but could not help mar-
velling at their opium-engendered fanaticism . . .

At last the guest began undressing, and Mr.
Golyadkin, imagining in his goodness of heart
that he might not have a proper shirt, disappeared
behind the partition, partly to avoid embarrassing
his guest, who had suffered quite enough already,
and partly to reassure himself as far as possible
about Petrushka, to sound him, cheer him up if
possible and be nice to him, so that everyone

should be happy, and that there should be no ill feeling. Petrushka, it must be observed, still made Mr. Golyadkin feel a bit uncomfortable.

'You get along to bed now, Petrushka,' said Mr. Golyadkin gently, walking into his servant's room. 'Go to bed now, Pyotr, and wake me tomorrow at eight, will you?'

Mr. Golyadkin's voice had been unusually soft and tender. But Petrushka remained silent. He was fussing about by his bed, and didn't even turn to face his master, as he should have done merely out of respect.

'Do you hear what I say, Pyotr?' continued Mr. Golyadkin. 'Go to bed now, and tomorrow wake me at eight. Is that clear?'

'I've got a memory, haven't I?' muttered Petrushka under his breath.

'Now now, Petruskha. I'm only telling you so that you can be happy and easy in your mind. We're all happy now, and you should be happy and contented too. And now I wish you good night. Get some sleep Petrushka, get some sleep. We all have our work to do. And don't you go thinking anything . . .'

Mr. Golyadkin left his sentence unfinished.

'Haven't I said a bit too much?' he thought. 'Haven't I gone too far? It's always the same. I always overdo it.'

Feeling very dissatisfied with himself, our hero left Petrushka. Apart from anything else, he had

been rather hurt by the latter's rudeness and in-
tractability.

'You're nice to him—you show him some
respect, and the scoundrel doesn't appreciate it.
Still, they've all got the same nasty way, that
sort!' thought Mr. Golyadkin.

Rather unsteadily he made his way back to his
room, and seeing that his guest had turned in,
sat down beside his bed for a minute.

'Come on, own up, Yasha,' he began in a
whisper, wagging his head. 'You're the one who's
in the wrong, aren't you, you rascal? You've got
my name, you know . . .' he went on, bantering
his guest in a rather familiar manner.

At last, bidding him a friendly good night, Mr.
Golyadkin retired to bed. The guest began to
snore. As Mr. Golyadkin climbed between the
sheets, he chuckled and whispered to himself:
'You're drunk tonight, Yakov Petrovich old boy.
What a rascal you are. Poor old Golyadkin!
And what's it you've been so pleased about?
Tomorrow it'll be all tears—you're a proper one
for snivelling. What's to be done with you?'

At this moment a rather peculiar sensation of
something approaching doubt or remorse per-
vaded his whole being.

'I let myself go,' he thought, 'and now my
brain's fuddled, and I'm drunk. I didn't keep a
grip on myself. What a fool I am! I talked a
string of nonsense when I meant to be cunning.

To forgive and forget is the first of all virtues, of course, but it's bad all the same! It is!"

Here Mr. Golyadkin got up, and taking a candle, tiptoed to have another look at his sleeping guest. For a long time he stood over him, deep in thought.

'Not a very pleasant picture! Sheer lampoonery —and that's all you can say about it!'

Finally Mr. Golyadkin went to bed. His brain was fuddled. His head was splitting. Gradually he began to doze . . . There was something he was trying hard to think of and remember, some very important and extremely ticklish matter he was trying to decide, but could not. Sleep descended upon his poor unfortunate head, and, as is customary with those who, being unused to it, suddenly consume five glasses of punch in a friendly evening, he was dead to the world.

## 8

Next day Mr. Golyadkin woke as usual at eight, instantly remembered all that had happened the night before, and frowned.

'I let myself go like a proper fool yesterday,' he thought, raising himself a little to take a look at his guest's bed. But imagine his amazement to find not only the guest but also the bed on which he had slept, gone from the room!

'What's this?' he almost shrieked. 'What's happened? What does this new thing mean?'

While Mr. Golyadkin was staring perplexed and open-mouthed at the empty space, the door creaked and in came Petrushka, bearing the tea-tray.

'Where is he? Where is he?' said our hero in a barely audible voice, pointing at the place that had been given over to the guest the previous night. Petrushka did not reply or even look at his master at first, but directed his gaze at the right-hand corner of the room, obliging Mr. Golyadkin to do likewise. Then, after a silence, he replied rather gruffly that his master was not at home.

'*I'm* your master, Petrushka, you fool!' faltered Mr. Golyadkin, staring open-eyed at his servant.

Petrushka made no answer, but cast an offen-
sively reproachful look at Mr. Golyadkin that was
tantamount to a piece of downright abuse, and
made him go as red as a beetroot. Mr. Golyadkin
gave up, as the saying is. At length Petrushka
announced that *the other* had left about an hour
and a half ago, not wishing to wait. This of course
was both probable and plausible. Clearly Petrushka was not lying, and his offensive look and
use of the words 'the other' were merely a result
of the whole odious occurrence of which we have
heard. All the same Mr. Golyadkin realized, albeit
vaguely, that there was something not quite right
about it, and that fate had something else in store
for him.

'Very well, we'll see,' he thought. 'We'll see,
and in due course we'll get to the bottom of it
all.'

'Oh God,' he moaned, his voice now quite
different. 'Why did I invite him here? What was
the point? I'm sticking my neck right into their
noose, and pulling the rope tight myself. Oh,
what a fool I am. I've got no restraint. I go blab-
bing away like a kid, like some miserable clerk,
like someone with no position to think of, like
some gutless, weak-willed creature! What a gossip, what an old woman I am! Saints above! He
wrote verses, the rascal, and said how he liked me!
What's the best way of showing him the door if
he comes back, I wonder? There are lots of ways

of putting it, of course. I could say that with my
limited salary and so forth . . . Or frighten him
up a bit and say that taking such and such into
consideration, I'm obliged to ask him to pay half
the rent and half the cost of food in advance.
Oh damn it! That's no good. That's giving
myself a bad name. It's not quite the thing.
Perhaps I could tip off Petrushka to be nasty to
him or slight him in some way, or be rude to
him, and get him out like that? Set one off against
the other. No, blast it! That's risky, and looked
at from another point of view, it's not very nice.
Not nice at all. And supposing he *doesn't* come?
That'll be bad too. I let my tongue run away
with me yesterday. It's a bad state of things. Very
bad indeed. What a damned fool I am! I just
can't hammer any sense into my head. What if
he comes and won't agree? I hope to God he
does come. I'd be jolly glad—I'd give a lot if he
would.'

Such were Mr. Golyadkin's thoughts as he
gulped his tea, keeping an eye on the clock.

'Quarter to nine. Time to be off. Something's
going to happen, but what? I'd like to know
what's behind all this—the aim and object, and
what the various snags are. It would be nice to
know what these people are trying to get at, and
what their first step is going to be . . .'

Mr. Golyadkin could bear it no longer, and
leaving his pipe half smoked, he dressed and set

off for the office, desiring, if possible, to take the source of danger by surprise, and to satisfy himself about everything at first hand. There *was* danger. He knew it.

'Now we'll find out all about it,' he said, removing his coat and galoshes in the entrance hall. 'Now we'll go into it.'

Having thus decided on a course of action, our hero straightened his jacket, and, assuming a correct and official air, was about to pass into the next room, when suddenly, right in the doorway, he came face to face with his friend and acquaintance of the day before. Golyadkin junior seemed not to notice him, even though they practically bumped noses. He was, it seemed, busy. He was dashing off somewhere, and was out of breath. His expression was official and business-like: 'On a special errand,' it said for all to see.

'Oh, it's you, Yakov Petrovich,' said our hero, seizing him by the hand.

'Not now, not now. Excuse me. You can tell me later,' cried Golyadkin junior, bursting forward.

'But excuse me, Yakov Petrovich. I believe you, er . . .'

'What's that? Hurry up. What's it about?' Here Mr. Golyadkin's guest halted as though it were an effort and against his will to do so, and stuck an ear right in front of Mr. Golyadkin's face.

'I'm surprised at your behaviour, Yakov Petrovich, I must say. It's not what I should have expected at all.'

'There's a proper form for doing everything. Apply to his Excellency through his Excellency's secretary in the proper way. Got a petition?'

'Really, Yakov Petrovich! You astound me! Perhaps you don't recognize me, or perhaps in your usual jolly way you are joking.'

'Oh, it's you!' said Golyadkin junior, as if only now seeing and recognising Golyadkin senior. 'So it's you. Well, did you have a good night?'

Here Golyadkin junior gave a little smile, a formal official smile, not at all like the one he should have given, since at all events he owed Golyadkin senior a debt of gratitude, and added that he was extremely glad the latter had had a good night. Then he bowed slightly, took a few quick steps, looked left, right, and then at the floor, made for the door at his side, and with a muttered 'special business,' slipped into the next room, and was gone.

'There's a nice thing for you!' whispered our hero, momentarily stunned. 'There's a nice thing! So that's how it is.' He felt his flesh creep.

'Still, I've been saying that for a long time,' he continued as he made his way to his section. 'I had a presentiment ages ago about his being on special business. I said as much only yesterday.'

'Have you finished that document you were

doing yesterday? Have you got it here?' asked Anton Antonovich Setochkin as Mr. Golyadkin took his seat beside him.

'It's here,' whispered Mr. Golyadkin, regarding his chief clerk with a rather lost expression.

'Ah yes. I only mention it because his Excellency has asked for it twice already. I'm afraid he'll ask again any minute.'

'It's all right. It's ready.'

'Oh well, that's all right then.'

'I have, I believe, always performed my duties properly, Anton Antonovich, taken care over the tasks entrusted to me by my superiors, and dealt with them assiduously.'

'Yes. But what do you mean by that?'

'Nothing, Anton Antonovich. I only want to explain that I . . . That is, I was trying to say that sometimes no one is spared, as ill-will and envy seek their noisome daily bread . . .'

'Forgive me, I don't quite follow you. Who are you getting at now?'

'All I mean, Anton Antonovich, is that I keep to the straight path and scorn beating about the bush. I'm not one for intrigue, and that, if you'll allow me to say so, is something I can very justly be proud of.'

'Yes. Quite so. And as I understand it, I concede the full justice of what you say. But allow me to point out to you, Yakov Petrovich, that remarks about other people are not allowed

in good society; and that I, for example, can put
up with what goes on behind my back, but will
permit no one to be impertinent to my face, sir.
I, sir, have grown grey in the service, and will
allow no one to be impertinent to me in my old
age!'

'No Anton Antonovich, you see . . . You
don't seem to have quite taken my meaning.
Good gracious, Anton Antonovich, I personally
can only account it an honour . . .'

'In that case I beg your pardon too. I've been
brought up in the old school. It's a bit late for
me to go learning your new ways. I've had
enough wit to serve my country up to now. I
hold, as you are aware, sir, a medal for twenty-
five years' unblemished service . . .'

'I know, Anton Antonovich, I fully realize all
that. But that's not what I was getting at. I was
talking about a mask, Anton Antonovich.'

'A mask?'

'That is, you again . . . I'm afraid you'll take
it the wrong way—the sense of what I say, that
is—as you yourself put it. I'm merely developing
the theme, putting forward the idea that people
who wear masks are no longer uncommon, and
that it's difficult nowadays to recognize the man
underneath.'

'It's not so hard as all that, you know. Sometimes it's fairly easy. Sometimes you don't have
to go far to find him.'

'No, Anton Antonovich. Speaking of myself for instance, I only put on a mask in the literal sense when there's some call to—when there's a carnival or a merry gathering; I don't, in a more cryptic sense, go about in one every day.'

'Oh well, let's leave it at that for now. I haven't got time . . .' said Anton Antonovich, rising from his seat, and gathering up some papers he was to report on to his Excellency. 'I don't suppose it'll be long before this affair of yours is cleared up. You'll see yourself who to blame and who to accuse, and I must ask you to spare me any further explanations and discussions to the detriment of the work.'

'No, Anton Antonovich. That's not what I was thinking . . .' began Mr. Golyadkin, paling slightly. But Anton Antonovich was walking away.

'What is it?' he continued, now to himself. 'Which way is the wind blowing now? What does it mean, this new piece of pettifoggery?'

Just as our dazed, half-annihilated hero was preparing to solve this new question, there was a sudden noise and burst of activity in the next room. The door opened, and there, quite out of breath, stood Andrey Filippovich, who a short time before had betaken himself to his Excellency on some matter. He called Mr. Golyadkin, and the latter realizing what it was about and not wishing to keep him waiting, sprang up, and as was fitting, made a great fuss about getting the required papers tidy and in order preparatory to following both them and Andrey Filippovich to his Excellency's room. Suddenly, and from practically under the arm of Andrey Filippovich, who was standing right in the doorway, in shot Golyadkin junior. He was breathless, he appeared exhausted by his official labours, and he had an earnest and decidedly formal air about him. He came bustling into the room, and marched straight up to Golyadkin senior—the very last thing the latter had expected.

'The papers, Yakov Petrovich, the papers, his Excellency has been pleased to inquire if you've got them ready,' gabbled Mr. Golyadkin's friend under his breath. 'Andrey Filippovich is waiting.'

'I know without your telling me,' shot back Golyadkin senior, also in a low voice.

'No, I didn't mean that. I didn't mean that at all, Yakov Petrovich. I feel for you, and I'm prompted by genuine concern.'

'Spare me your concern, I beg you. Now, excuse me.'

'Of course, you'll put them in a folder, Yakov Petrovich, and insert a page as a marker. Allow me, Yakov Petrovich . . .'

'No. Allow me, please . . .'

'But there's a blot here, Yakov Petrovich. Did you notice it?'

At that moment Andrey Filippovich called Mr. Golyadkin for the second time.

'Coming, Andrey Filippovich. I've just got to . . .' Then to Golyadkin junior: 'Can't you understand plain language, sir?'

'The best thing is to get it out with a penknife, Yakov Petrovich. You'd better leave it to me. Best not touch it yourself, Yakov Petrovich. Leave it to me. I'll get it out.'

Andrey Filippovich called Mr. Golyadkin for the third time.

'Where is it, for goodness' sake? I can't see any blot.'

'It's an enormous one. Look, here's where I saw it. Just allow me, Yakov Petrovich. I'll do it with a pen-knife. I'll do it out of friendship and pure goodness of heart. . . . There! That's done it.'

Getting the better of Golyadkin senior in the momentary struggle that had arisen between them, Golyadkin junior at this point suddenly, quite unexpectedly, for no apparent reason, and quite against the other's will, seized the document required by their chief, and instead of attending to it with a pen-knife, 'out of pure goodness of heart' as he had perfidiously assured Golyadkin senior, he quickly rolled it up, thrust it under his arm, and in two bounds was at the side of Andrey Filippovich; the latter having noticed none of his pranks, shot off with him to the Director's room.

Mr. Golyadkin stood glued to the spot, a pen-knife in his hand, looking as if he was getting ready to scratch something out with it.

He had not yet grasped what had happened to him, or gathered his senses. He had felt a sudden blow, but thought it was nothing serious. Filled with indescribable anguish, he at last tore himself away, and rushed straight off to the Director's room, praying to heaven as he went that the whole thing might somehow turn out for the best, and be all right. With one room still to go, he came face to face with Andrey Filippovich and Golyadkin junior, who were both on their way back. Andrey Filippovich was smiling and talking gaily. Mr. Golyadkin's namesake was also smiling. He was trotting along, keeping a respectful distance from Andrey Filippovich, but playing up to him and whispering delightedly into his ear, while the latter affably nodded assent. Our hero saw the whole situation in a flash. His work, as he discovered later, had exceeded his Excellency's expectations, and had, in fact, been delivered by the time appointed. His Excellency had been most gratified, and had, it was even rumoured, thanked Golyadkin junior, thanked him warmly and said he would bear it in mind when the time came, and wouldn't forget. The first thing for Mr. Golyadkin to do, of course, was to protest with the utmost possible vigour. Pale as death and almost out of his mind, he rushed up to

Andrey Filippovich. But the latter, hearing that
Mr. Golyadkin's business was of a personal nature,
refused to listen, remarking bluntly that he hadn't
a minute to spare for his own requirements. His
flat refusal and matter-of-fact tone left Mr.
Golyadkin dumbfounded.

'I'd better go about it a different way. I'd
better go to Anton Antonovich,' he thought.

Unfortunately for Mr. Golyadkin Anton Antonovich was not available. He was also busy
somewhere.

'So there was some purpose in his asking to be
spared discussions and explanations,' thought our
hero. 'So that's what he was getting at, the cunning old devil! In that case I'll simply be bold
and petition his Excellency.'

Still pale, feeling his head to be in a state of
complete chaos, and at an utter loss what to
decide on next, Mr. Golyadkin sat down on his
chair.

'It would have been much better if it had all
been a mere nothing,' he kept thinking to himself. 'Anything as black as this was really quite
inconceivable. It's nonsense. It can't happen. It's
probably been some sort of an illusion—either
something different happened from what actually
did—or it was me who went, and somehow I
took myself for someone else. To put it briefly,
the whole thing is impossible.'

No sooner had Mr. Golyadkin decided that the

whole thing was impossible, than all of a sudden
Golyadkin junior came flying into the room, with
papers in both hands and under both arms. Saying
a few needful words to Andrey Filippovich as he
passed, exchanging a remark or two with one,
civilities with another and banter with a third,
Golyadkin junior, having apparently not a moment to waste, seemed just on the point of going
out again, when, fortunately for Golyadkin senior,
he stopped by the door to have a word in passing
with two or three young clerks who happened to
be standing there. Golyadkin senior hurled himself forward. Noticing this, Golyadkin junior
began looking round uneasily to see how to make
good his escape. But Mr. Golyadkin had already
got him by the sleeve. The clerks surrounding
the two officials stepped back to give them room,
and stood inquisitively awaiting events. Golyadkin senior realized only too well that opinion was
not now disposed in his favour, and that he was
the victim of intrigue. This made it all the more
necessary that he should now stand up for himself.
It was a decisive moment.

'Well?' inquired Golyadkin junior, looking
rather impudently at him.

Golyadkin senior was barely breathing.

'I don't know how you can explain your
strange behaviour to me now, sir,' he began.

'Well, go on.' Here Golyadkin junior looked
around and winked at the surrounding clerks as

if giving them to understand that the comedy would now begin.

'The impertinent and shameless manner in which you have treated me in the present instance, exposes your true nature better than any words of mine could do. I shouldn't rely on the game you're playing. It's not a very good one.'

'Tell me, what sort of a night did you spend, Yakov Petrovich?' asked Golyadkin junior, looking him straight in the eye.

'You're forgetting yourself, sir!' said our hero, utterly flabbergasted, hardly knowing whether he was on his head or his heels. 'I trust you will change your tone.'

'There, my dear chap!' said Golyadkin junior, making a rather improper grimace at Golyadkin senior, and all of a sudden, moving as if to caress him, he pinched his chubby cheek. Our hero flushed scarlet. As soon as he saw that his adversary, now speechless with rage, red as a lobster, and shaking in every limb, had been driven to breaking point and might attempt an assault, Golyadkin junior at once forestalled him in a most shameless manner. After playing with him a few seconds more, patting his cheeks and tickling him in the ribs while he stood motionless and out of his mind with rage, Golyadkin junior, to the huge delight of the young men standing around, and with an effrontery that was nothing short of disgusting, finished by giving Golyadkin senior a prod in his rather prominent stomach, and saying with an insinuating and positively malicious leer:

'You're a tricky one you are, Yakov Petrovich old chap. We'll fox 'em, you and I.'

Then, before our hero had time to make even a partial recovery, Golyadkin junior, after a preliminary grin at his audience, assumed a most brisk, business-like and official air, drew himself in, and with a rapid 'on a special errand', jerked his stumpy little legs into life, and darted off into the next room. Our hero could not believe his eyes. He was still in no state to regain his senses.

At last he recovered. Realizing in a flash that he was done for, that he had in a manner of speaking destroyed himself, that he had been disgraced, that his reputation was ruined, and that he had been scorned and ridiculed in front of others—realizing that he had been perfidiously abused by him he had considered his greatest and most trusty friend, and finally, realizing that he had been utterly shamed, Mr. Golyadkin charged in pursuit of his enemy. He tried not to think of those who had witnessed the outrage.

'They're all hand in glove together,' he said to himself. 'They all back each other up, and one sets the other against me.'

Seeing after a dozen steps, however, that pursuit was in vain, he turned back.

'You won't get away!' he thought. 'I'll beat

you in good time. You'll pay for all the misery you've caused!'

Filled with cold fury and violent determination, he went to his chair and sat down.

'You won't get away,' he repeated.

Any form of passive defence was now out of the question. There was something decisive, something of an offensive in the air, and anyone who at that moment saw Mr. Golyadkin, flushed and hardly able to control his agitation, jab his pen into the inkstand, and saw the fury with which he started scribbling on the paper, could have told that the matter would not be allowed to pass and end in some old-womanish way. In his heart of hearts he had formed a resolution which in his heart of hearts he had sworn to carry out. To be truthful, he still did not quite know or rather, he had no idea what steps to take. But it didn't matter.

'Imposture and effrontery, sir, get you nowhere today. Imposture and effrontery, sir, lead to no good. They lead to destruction. The False Demetrius was the only one to gain by imposture, sir—after deceiving a blind people—but not for long.'

In spite of this Mr. Golyadkin thought he would wait for the masks to fall from certain faces, and one or two things to come to light. The first requisite was that office hours should end as quickly as possible, and until they did, he proposed to do nothing. When office hours were over, he would take a certain step. After that he would know how to act, and how to plan his whole campaign to shatter the horn of arrogance and crush the serpent, as in impotent rage it gnawed the dust. He could not allow anyone to wipe their dirty boots with him. He could not agree to that, particularly in the present case. But for the last humiliation, our hero might have swallowed his feelings, said nothing, and given in without too stubborn a protest; he would have argued a bit, taken slight offence, aired a few grievances, proved himself in the right, and then would have climbed down a little; he might perhaps have climbed down a little further, and then agreed entirely; then, and especially then, when the other party solemnly acknowledged him to be in the right, he might even have made peace and displayed a little emotion; and who knows, a new friendship might have been born— a firm, warm friendship on a broader basis than that of the preceding evening—a friendship that might finally have so eclipsed the unpleasantness of the rather improper resemblance between them, that both would have known unbounded delight and lived to be a hundred, and so on.

To tell all, Mr. Golyadkin was beginning rather to regret that he had stuck up for himself and his rights when disagreeableness had been his immediate reward.

'If he'd give in, and say it was a joke, I'd for-give him,' thought Mr. Golyadkin. 'I'd forgive him all the more if he'd only admit it out loud. But I won't be used as a boot-rag. I haven't allowed others to wipe their boots with me, and that's all the more reason for not letting some depraved fellow try to do so. I'm not a boot-rag, sir. I'm not!'

Our hero had in short made up his mind:

'You yourself are the guilty one, sir!'

He had made up his mind to protest with all his power and to the uttermost. That was the sort of man he was! He could not permit himself to be insulted, still less to be used as a boot-rag by someone depraved.

But let there be no argument about it. Per-haps if anyone had wanted—had suddenly felt a desire to turn Mr. Golyadkin into a boot-rag, they could have done so with impunity, encoun-tering no resistance—Mr. Golyadkin had occasion-ally sensed that himself—and a boot-rag there would have been, and not a Golyadkin; a nasty dirty boot-rag, it's true, but still no ordinary one; this boot-rag would have had pride, would have been alive and had feelings; pride and feelings might have remained concealed deep in its filthy folds and been unable to speak for themselves, but all the same they would have been there.

The hours seemed incredibly long, but at last it struck four. A few minutes later everyone got

up, and following out their departmental head,
made for home. Mr. Golyadkin mingled with
the crowd, keeping his quarry in sight. He saw
him dash up to the porters who were handing
out the overcoats, and stand ingratiating himself
with them in his usual blackguardly way while
waiting for his. The moment had come. Somehow Mr. Golyadkin pushed his way through the
crowd and tried to get his overcoat, not wishing
to be left behind. But the first to be served was
Mr. Golyadkin's friend, for here too he had
managed in his own inimitable fashion to wheedle
and whisper his way round people.

Flinging on his coat, Golyadkin junior glanced
ironically at Golyadkin senior, spiting him boldly
and openly. Then, surveying all around with an
impudence peculiarly his own, he made a last
rapid round of the clerks—probably so as to
leave them with a good impression—having a
word with one and a whisper with another,
oozing respect to a third, smiling at a fourth, giving
his hand to a fifth—and finally darted gaily down
the steps. Golyadkin senior followed. To his
indescribable delight he overtook Golyadkin junior
on the last step, and seized him by the coat-collar.
Golyadkin junior seemed a little scared and looked
round with a bewildered expression.

'What do you mean by this?' he said in a half-
whisper.

'If, sir, you are a gentleman, I trust you will

recollect our cordial relationship of yesterday,'
said our hero.

'Ah, yes. Well, did you have a good night?'

For the moment Golyadkin senior was speechless with rage.

'Yes I did. But let me tell you, it's a com-
plicated game you're playing.'

'Who says so?—My enemies!' retorted the
self-styled Mr. Golyadkin, breaking away from
the feeble grasp of the real one. Once free, he
dashed away, and catching sight of a cab, rushed
up to it, climbed in, and a moment later was out
of sight.

Abandoned by all and filled with despair, our
minor civil servant gazed around, but there was
no other cab. He tried to run, but his legs bent
beneath him. Looking utterly downcast, his
mouth sagging open, he leant against a lamp-post,
feeling shrivelled up and finished. And thus for
several minutes he remained, in the middle of
the pavement. For Mr. Golyadkin all seemed
lost . . .

## 9

Everything, even Nature herself, seemed to be up in arms against Mr. Golyadkin. But he was still on his feet and unbeaten. He was ready to do battle. He would not give in—so much was plain from the spirit and vigour with which he rubbed his hands on recovering from the first of his amazement. But danger, obvious danger was upon him. He sensed it. Yet how to tackle it?—that was the question.

'Why not leave it like this? Why not just break with him without any formality?' flashed across his mind.

'Why not? There's nothing to it. I'll keep to myself as if it isn't me. I'll let it all pass. It isn't me, and that's all there is to it. He'll also keep to himself. Maybe he'll break with me. He'll be all over me for a bit, the wretch, then he'll turn round and break with me. That's how it will be. I'll triumph through meekness. Where's the danger in that? What danger is there? I'd just like someone to show me. It's a mere nothing. The sort of thing that happens every day!' Here Mr. Golyadkin stopped short. The words died on his lips. He cursed himself for thinking such thoughts, and accused himself of being mean and cowardly.

However, his cause was still no further advanced. To make some sort of decision at this moment was, he felt, a matter of absolute necessity. But he would have given a lot to anyone who could have told him what exactly the decision should be. How was he to find out? Still, there was no time for that now. To avoid wasting any more time he took a cab and hastened homewards.

'Well? How are you feeling now?' he thought to himself. 'How are you feeling now, Yakov Petrovich? What will you do? What will you do now, you abject wretch? You brought yourself to this, and now you're snivelling and crying!' Thus did Mr. Golyadkin taunt himself as he jogged up and down in his rickety cab. He derived considerable pleasure from turning the knife in his wound in this fashion—there was something almost voluptuous about it.

'If some magician were to come along now,' he thought, 'or if it were put to me in some official sort of way: "You give a finger of your right hand, Golyadkin, and we'll be quits. There won't be any *other Golyadkin,* and you'll be happy but minus a finger"—I'd give it willingly, without a murmur.'

'Damn and blast it all!' he cried at last in despair. 'What's it all for? Why did this of all things have to happen? As if nothing else were possible! And it was all all right at first. Everyone was happy and content. But no, this had to happen! Still, talking won't get me anywhere. Action is what's needed.'

With this much decided, Mr. Golyadkin, once back in his rooms, grabbed his pipe without a moment's delay, and sucking away at it as hard as he could and emitting clouds of smoke to left and right, began pacing to and fro in extreme agitation. Meanwhile Petrushka started laying the table. Suddenly, his mind at last made up, Mr. Golyadkin threw down his pipe, dragged on his overcoat, and announcing that he would not be in for dinner, charged out. On the stairs, he was caught up by Petrushka, panting for breath and holding the hat he had forgotten. Mr. Golyadkin took it, and meant to say something about 'There! I forgot my hat' by way of justifying himself, and to stop Petrushka thinking anything out of the ordinary; but as the latter did not so much as look at him and immediately went back, he put on his hat without more ado, and ran downstairs, repeating to himself that everything might be for the best and that the business would be settled somehow, although he was conscious amongst other things of a nasty chill sensation all over him. He went into the street, took a cab, and shot off to Andrey Filippovich's.

'Wouldn't tomorrow be better?' he wondered, reaching for the bell-pull at the door of Andrey Filippovich's flat. 'Besides, have I got anything special to say? There's nothing special about it.

It's such a paltry business—it really is. It's paltry, piffling—or almost—the whole thing . . .'

Suddenly Mr. Golyadkin pulled the bell; it tinkled, and footsteps were heard within. At this juncture Mr. Golyadkin cursed himself for his boldness and precipitance. Certain recent distressing incidents, which he had almost forgotten while at work, and his misunderstanding with Andrey Filippovich, immediately recurred to him. But it was too late for flight. The door opened. As good luck would have it, Mr. Golyadkin was informed that Andrey Filippovich had not returned from the office, and was dining out.

'I know where—by the Izmaylovsky Bridge—that's where he dines,' thought our hero, overjoyed. On the footman inquiring what message he would leave, he replied, 'Oh, that's all right. I'll pop back later, my man,' and ran down the stairs with an almost jaunty air. In the street he decided to dismiss the cab, and settled with the driver. When the latter solicited a tip, pleading that he had had a long wait and hadn't spared his horse for the gentleman, he gave him an extra five kopeks quite cheerfully, and then set off on foot.

'Really it's the sort of business you can't just leave like that,' thought Mr. Golyadkin. 'But if you think about it—if you really think about it sensibly, what actually is the point of fussing about here?—No. I still repeat what I've said—why should *I* have all the bother? Why should I kill myself, toiling, worrying and making all the effort? What's done can't be undone, for a start. It can't! We'll argue it this way: along comes a man with adequate references, a capable clerk, well-behaved, but badly-off—had an unpleasant time of it one way and other—been some trouble. Well, poverty's no crime. It's nothing to do with me. What's all the nonsense about then? It so happens that Nature has made someone the spit and image, the exact replica, of someone else. Can you refuse to employ him because of that? If it's fate—if it's only fate or blind fortune that's to blame, how can you treat him like dirt and refuse him a job? What justice would there be after that? There he is, penniless, brow-beaten, forlorn. . . . Your heart aches for him. Fellow-feeling demands you should look after him. Fine people departmental heads would be if they argued the same way as a ruffian like me! What a brain I've got! Sometimes I'm as stupid as a dozen fools put together! No. They did well, and I say thank you to them for taking care of the poor wretch . . .

'Well, suppose for the sake of example that we are twins—twin brothers. What of it? Nothing! All the clerks can be got used to it. And no one coming in from outside would think there was anything unseemly or outrageous about it. It's rather touching even; divine Providence creates two identical beings, the beneficent authorities behold the divine handiwork, and here they are giving them a place of refuge. It would of course have been better,' went on Mr. Golyadkin, taking breath and lowering his voice, 'if there'd been none of this touching business, and no twins either . . . Why did it have to be, blast it! What particular and urgent necessity was there for it? God! What a damned mess! Look at the sort of person he is! He's frivolous and beastly. He's a blackguard. He's here there and everywhere. He's a toady and a lick-spittle. That's the sort of Golyadkin he is! He'll misbehave some more, I shouldn't wonder, and drag my name in the mud, the scoundrel. And now I've got to look after him and humour him, if you please! What a punishment! Still, what of it? It doesn't matter. He's a blackguard. Well, suppose he is—the other Mr. Golyadkin's straight. He'll be the blackguard, and I'll be the honest one, and people will say, "That Golyadkin's a blackguard. Don't you take any notice of him, and don't mix him up with the other one who's honest, virtuous, gentle and forgiving, who's very reliable at work and deserves promotion." That's it! All right, then . . . But . . . But what if they do get us mixed? He's capable of anything. Oh God! He's the sort of blackguard who'll deliberately take your place as though you were just dirt. He won't stop to think that you're not. Oh God! What horrible luck!'

Reasoning and complaining thus, Mr. Golyadkin scuttled along, heedless and almost unaware of
where he was going. He came to in the Nevsky
Prospect, and then only by virtue of a head-on
collision with someone, that made him see stars.
He muttered an apology, keeping his head lowered,
and only when the other, after growling something uncomplimentary was well on his way
again, did he raise it to see where he was and how
he had got there. Finding himself to be right by
the restaurant in which he had taken his ease prior
to the dinner-party at Olsufy Ivanovich's, he became suddenly conscious of a rumbling and
rattling in his stomach, and remembered he had
not dined. There was no prospect of a dinner-
party anywhere, and so, without losing precious
time, he darted up the stairs and into the restaurant,
to snatch a quick bite of something to avoid delay.
The restaurant was rather on the expensive side,
but that did not stop Mr. Golyadkin. There was
no time to stop over trifles like that now. In the
brightly illuminated room, quite a crowd of customers was standing at a counter heaped with an
assortment of all the good things that respectable
people might consume by way of light refresh-
ment. The waiter was hard put to it, filling
glasses, serving, taking money and giving change.
Mr. Golyadkin waited, and as soon as his turn
came, reached modestly for a fish pasty. Retiring
to a corner and turning his back on the company,

he ate with relish. When he had finished he went and returned his plate, and knowing the price, left a ten-kopek piece on the counter, catching the waiter's eye to let him know he'd had one fish pasty and had left the money, etc.

'That'll be one rouble ten kopeks,' said the waiter contemptuously.

Mr. Golyadkin was amazed.

'What's that you say? I-I've only had one, I think.'

'You've had eleven,' retorted the waiter with conviction.

'I think you're making a mistake. I took one, I assure you.'

'Eleven you took. I counted. You must pay for what you've had. We don't give stuff away.'

Mr. Golyadkin was stupefied. 'What's happening to me? Is it some piece of wizardry?' he thought. The man stood waiting for him to make up his mind. A crowd had gathered. Mr. Golyadkin slipped his hand into his pocket for a rouble, meaning to square up at once and avoid further trouble.

'If he says eleven, eleven it is,' he thought, turning a lobster red. 'Well, what's wrong with eating eleven pasties? If a chap's hungry and eats eleven pasties, well, let him, and good luck to him. There's nothing funny or wonderful about that . . .'

Feeling a sudden stabbing pain in his side, he looked up. The mystery, the wizardry became

suddenly clear.  He was perplexed no longer . . .
Standing in the doorway of the next room, almost
directly behind the waiter and facing Mr. Golyadkin—standing in the doorway, which till then he
had taken to be a mirror—was a little man.  It
was Mr. Golyadkin, not Golyadkin the elder, the
hero of our tale, but the other, the new Golyadkin,
and evidently in the best of spirits.  He kept
smiling, nodding and winking at Golyadkin I,
shifting restlessly from one foot to the other, and
looking as though he might at the least provoca-
tion disappear into the next room and slip out by
a back way, foiling all attempts at pursuit.  He held
in his hand the last morsel of his tenth pasty, and
this, before Mr. Golyadkin's very eyes, he consigned
to his mouth, smacking his lips with enjoyment.

'He's passed himself off as me, the blackguard!'
thought Mr. Golyadkin, flushing red with shame.
'He's got no qualms about other people being
present!  Can they see him?  I don't think so.'

Mr. Golyadkin threw down the rouble as
though it burnt his fingers, and without noticing
the waiter's insolent smile of triumph and cool
mastery, broke out of the crowd, and dashed off,
not daring to look back.

'Thank goodness he at least didn't compromise
anyone completely,' he thought.  'Thanks are due
to him, the villain, and to fate that it still got
settled all right.  There was just the cheekiness of
the waiter.  Still, he was within his rights.  It

should have been one rouble ten kopeks, so he was within his rights. "We don't give stuff away," he said. He could have been a bit more polite about it though—the horrible man!'

All this Mr. Golyadkin said to himself as he made his way downstairs to the street-door. On the last step, however, he stopped dead in his tracks, his face grew suddenly red and tears started to his eyes as he suffered a paroxysm of injured pride. After standing motionless for half a minute, he gave a determined stamp, bounded out into the street, and panting for breath and unconscious of his weariness, he headed for Shestilavochnaya Street and home without once looking back. As soon as he was indoors he seated himself on the ottoman, still wearing his overcoat—which was quite contrary to his custom of making himself comfortable in his own house—and without even observing the preliminary of reaching for a pipe, drew the inkstand towards him, took a pen and a sheet of notepaper, and began, his hand trembling with suppressed excitement, to scribble the following missive.

Dear Yakov Petrovich,

I should never have taken up my pen, had not circumstances, and you yourself, sir, compelled me to do so. Believe me when I say that necessity alone has obliged me to embark upon explanations with you, and I beg above all, sir, that you will regard this not as a deliberate attempt to insult you, but as an inevitable consequence of those things which are now a link between us.

'I think that's all right—polite and proper—although at the same time, firm and forceful. . . . I don't think there's anything for him to take exception to there.  Besides, I'm within my rights,' thought Mr. Golyadkin, reading over what he had written.

Your appearance, sir, singular and unheralded on a tempestuous night, following upon coarse and unseemly conduct towards me on the part of my enemies, whose names I shall not mention for the contempt I bear them, was the genesis of all those misapprehensions which at present exist between us.  Your persistence in forcing an entry into the circle of my existence, and into all my relationships in practical life, exceeds the bounds dictated by common courtesy and social custom.  There is, I think, little need to remind you here of your appropriation of papers of mine, together with my own good name, for the purpose of currying favour with those in authority—a favour you have not merited.  I need hardly make mention here of the offensive and calculating manner in which you have avoided tendering those explanations which these acts have rendered indispensable.  Finally, to withhold nothing from you, I do not allude to your

recent peculiar—one might almost say incomprehensible—behaviour towards me in the coffee
house. Far be it from me to complain of what
proved the needless expenditure of one rouble.
Nevertheless I cannot but vent my indignation at
the recollection of your flagrant attempt to pre-
judice my honour, and what is more, to do so in
the presence of several persons of breeding, albeit
not personal acquaintances of mine . . .

'Am I going too far?' wondered Mr. Golyadkin.
'Isn't it a bit strong? Isn't it being too touchy—
that hint about breeding for instance? No, it
doesn't matter! Firmness is the thing with him.
Still, to soften the blow, I can butter him up a bit
at the end. We'll see.'

I should not however be wearying you with
this letter, were I not firmly persuaded that your
nobility of heart and forthrightness will suggest
to you the means of rectifying all omissions and
restoring the status quo ante.
I venture to hope and trust that you will not
take this letter as offensive to yourself, and that at
the same time you will not decline to write explaining yourself—sending your reply by my
servant.

　　　　　In anticipation, I remain, Sir,
　　　　　　　Your obedient servant,
　　　　　　　　　Y. Golyadkin.

'There, that's all right. It's done now. It's got to the stage of letter-writing. But who's to thank for that? He is. He's the one who reduces you to the necessity of having something in writing. I'm within my rights.'

After reading over the letter for the last time, Mr. Golyadkin folded it, sealed it up, and summoned Petrushka, who appeared as usual looking bleary-eyed and extremely put out about something.

'I want you to take this letter. You understand?'

Petrushka remained silent.

'I want you to take it to the office, and find Vakhrameyev—he's duty secretary today. You understand?'

'Yes.'

'"Yes!" Can't you say, "Yes, sir"? Ask for Vakhrameyev, and tell him your master sends his compliments, and wonders if he would be so good as to look up the office address book and find where Golyadkin the clerk is living.'

Petrushka made no reply, and Mr. Golyadkin thought he detected him smiling.

'Well, that's it, then. Ask the address, and find out where Golyadkin the new clerk is living.'

'Right.'

'Ask the address, and then take this letter there, got it?'

'Yes.'

'If, when you get there, this gentleman you're taking the letter to—this Golyadkin . . . What are you laughing at, dolt?'

'Me? What have *I* got to laugh about? It's not for the likes of me to laugh.'

'Very well then . . . If this gentleman should ask how your master is, or how he's getting on or anything like that, you just keep your tongue to yourself, and say "My master's all right, and asks for a written reply." You understand?'

'Yes, sir.'

'Very well then. "My master's all right," you'll say. "He's quite fit and is just going visiting," you'll say. "And he asked for a written answer." Got that?'

'Yes.'

'Well, off you go.'

'What a job it is with this blockhead too! He just laughs. And what at? Things have come to a pretty pass! Still, perhaps it will all turn out for the best . . . The wretch will probably loiter about for a couple of hours now, then disappear somewhere. You can't send him anywhere. What a mess it is. What a mess!'

Being thus sensible of how full was the cup of his affliction, Mr. Golyadkin resolved to adopt a passive rôle for the two hours during which he should await Petrushka. For one of them he paced the room, smoking. Discarding his pipe, he sat down to a book. He had a short lie-down on the ottoman. He resumed his pipe. He began coursing about the room again. He tried to thrash things out, but found himself quite unable to do so. Finally, as the agony of remaining passive reached its peak, he made up his mind to do something.

'Petrushka will be back in an hour,' he thought. 'I can give the key to the porter, and go and, um . . . investigate on my own meanwhile.'

Losing no time in his haste to investigate, he took his hat and went out, locking up behind him. He handed the key to the porter together with a ten-kopek tip—he had become unusually liberal of late—and set off.

He headed first for the Izmaylovsky Bridge, a walk of half an hour or so. On arriving at his goal, he went straight into the courtyard of the house with which he was familiar, and glanced up at the windows of Civil Counsellor Berendeyev's apartments. All save three hung with red curtains were in darkness.

'I don't suppose Olsufy Ivanovich has got any visitors today,' thought Mr. Golyadkin. 'They're all at home on their own.'

He stood in the courtyard quite a while, trying to make a decision. But the decision was evidently fated to remain unmade, for suddenly he thought better of it, and with a wave of the hand returned to the street.

'No, I shouldn't have come here. What is there

for me to do here? I'd better go now, and, um, investigate in person.'

With that Mr. Golyadkin set off for the office. He had a long walk ahead of him, added to which it was dreadfully slushy underfoot, and great soggy flakes of snow were falling fast. But difficulties seemed not to exist for him. True, he was drenched to the skin and not a little bespattered with mud, but that was just by the way, provided his object were attained. And he was indeed nearing his goal. He could see the huge government building looming dark in the distance.

'Hold on!' he thought suddenly. 'Where am I going? And what am I going to do when I get there? Suppose I find out where he lives— Petrushka will have got back meanwhile with the answer. I shall just be wasting my valuable time for nothing, as I've done already. It doesn't matter, though. The whole thing can still be put right. But oughtn't I to go and see Vakhrameyev? No! I can do that afterwards. Confound it! I needn't have come out at all. But that's what I'm like. I've got a knack of trying to rush ahead whether there's any need to or not. Hm . . . What time is it? Nine, I suppose. Petrushka may get back and find me gone. I was a fool to come out. Oh, what a fuss and bother it is!'

After frankly admitting himself to have been a fool, our hero dashed back to Shestilavochnaya Street, and got there tired and exhausted. From the porter he learnt that Petrushka had not yet appeared. 'There! Just as I foresaw,' he thought. 'And it's nine already. What a useless thing he is. Always boozing somewhere. Oh, God! What a miserable day it's been for me!'

Reflecting and lamenting thus, Mr. Golyadkin let himself into his rooms. He got a candle, undressed, lit a pipe, and weak, weary, worn and hungry, lay down on the ottoman to await Petrushka. The candle burnt dimly. Its light flickered on the walls. He gazed thoughtfully into space, and finally fell dead asleep.

Late at night he awoke. The candle, which had burnt right down, was smoking and on the point of going out altogether. Mr. Golyadkin sprang to his feet, jerked himself into life, and remembered everything. Through the partition came the resonant snores of Petrushka. He rushed to the window—not a light anywhere. He opened the vent—not a sound. The city slept. It must therefore have been two or three in the morning. And indeed it was, for with a sudden effort the clock behind the partition struck two. Mr. Golyadkin charged into the next room.

Somehow after prolonged effort he roused Petrushka and succeeded in getting him to sit up in bed. At that precise moment the candle went out for good. It was about ten minutes before he found and lit another, and during that time Petrushka managed to drop off again.

'Blackguard! Villain!' shouted Mr. Golyadkin, rousing him once more. 'Get up! Wake up, will you!'

After half an hour's solid effort Mr. Golyadkin succeeded in stirring his servant into life, and dragging him into his own room. Only then did he see that Petrushka was, as the saying is, as drunk as a lord, and hardly able to stand.

'Lounger! Rogue!' cried Mr. Golyadkin. 'Shamed me, that's what you've done!

'Oh God! Where has he got rid of the letter? What's happened to it? And why did I write it? Was there any need? Like a damned fool I let myself get carried away by my pride. And this is where it's got me. So much for your pride!

'What have you done with the letter, you thief? Who did you give it to?'

'I didn't give any letter to anybody. I didn't have any letter. So there!'

Mr. Golyadkin wrung his hands in despair.

'Listen Pyotr, listen to me.'

'I'm listening.'

'Where've you been? Tell me.'

'To see nice people, that's where I've been. What do I care!'

'God help me! Where did you go first? The office? Listen Pyotr—perhaps you had a drop too much.'

'Me? Strike me dead on the spot—n-n-not a d-d-drop. So there!'

'It doesn't matter your being drunk, I was only asking. It's all right your being drunk. I don't mind, Petrushka, I don't mind. Perhaps you've just forgotten for a bit, but you'll remember. Now come on, try. Did you see the clerk Vakhrameyev, or not?'

'No. There wasn't any clerk. Strike me dead.'

'No, no, no, Petrushka. I don't mind, you know. You can see I don't. Well, then. It was cold out, and wet, so you had a quick one. I don't mind. I'm not angry. I had one today myself, old chap. Now come on, and try to remember, old fellow. Did you see Vakhrameyev?'

'Well, it was like this. Honest truth—I did go, straight I did . . .'

'That's fine, Petrushka. Fine. I'm not angry, you see,' continued our hero, coaxing his servant still more, patting him on the shoulder and smiling at him. 'So you had a quick one, you rogue? Ten kopeks' worth, eh? You bad man! Well, it doesn't matter. You can see I'm not angry. I'm not, old chap. I'm not at all.'

'I'm not a bad man. You can say what you like . . . Just because I went to see some nice people. I'm not a bad man, and I never have been.'

'No, Petrushka, of course not. Listen, Petrushka, I'm not scolding you, you know, when I call you a bad man. I mean it in a nice sense, to cheer you up. You know Petrushka, it's a compliment to some men, if you call them rogues or sly ones. It means they're no fools and don't let themselves get taken in. Some people like that. Well, never mind. Now, come on Petrushka. No beating about the bush. Tell me straight—like you would a friend. Did you go to Vakhrameyev and did he give you an address?'

'Yes, he did. He gave me that too. He's a nice official. "And your master's a nice man too," he said, "a very nice man." "And give your master my compliments," he said, "and thank him, and tell him how much I like and esteem him," he said. "For your master's a good man, Petrushka, and you're a good man too."'

'God give me strength! The address, the address, you Judas!' These last words he almost whispered.

'Yes, he gave me that.'

'He did? Well, where does he live, this Golyadkin?'

'"You'll find Golyadkin in Shestilavochnaya Street," he said. "As you walk down it, you'll see a staircase on the right, and it's the fourth floor. That's where you'll find Golyadkin," he said.'

'Swindler, cutthroat!' shouted our hero, finally losing all patience. 'That's me you're talking about. There's another Golyadkin, and I mean *him,* you twister!'

'Just as you like. I don't care. Have it your own way.'

'But the letter! The letter!'

'What letter? There wasn't any letter. I didn't see any letter.'

'What did you do with it, you crook?'

'Delivered it. "My compliments and thanks to him," he said. "He's a good man, your master. Give him my compliments," he said.'

'*Who* said? Golyadkin?'

For a moment Petrushka remained silent, then, staring his master straight in the face, he gave a broad smile.

'Listen, you villain!' began Mr. Golyadkin, breathless and losing his head in his fury. 'What have you done to me? Come on, tell me! Played me a filthy trick—landed me in the cart! You horrible wretch! You—Judas!'

'Have it your own way. What do I care?' said Petrushka firmly, retiring behind the partition.

'Come here! Come here, you idle fool!'

'Shan't now! Shan't! I don't care! I'm going to nice people. Nice people live honestly. Nice people don't live falsely and don't have doubles.'

Mr. Golyadkin's hands and feet turned to ice. He couldn't breathe.

'Yes,' continued Petrushka, 'they don't have doubles—ever. They aren't an insult to God and honest men.'

'You're drunk, you lazy lump! Sleep now, you

miserable thing, and tomorrow you'll get what's coming to you!' said Mr. Golyadkin, his voice almost a whisper. Petrushka muttered something else, and then could be heard making the bed creak as he lay down. He gave a prolonged yawn, stretched himself out, and finally began snoring away in what is called the sleep of the just.

Mr. Golyadkin felt more dead than alive. Petrushka's behaviour, his strange albeit vague insinuations—which were nothing to get annoyed about, especially as he had been drunk—and the whole ugly turn of things had shaken him to the core.

'Whatever possessed me to go for him in the middle of the night?' said our hero. A morbid sensation was causing him to tremble all over. 'Something egged me into getting tied up with him when he was drunk! What sense can you get out of anyone in that state! It's a lie every time he opens his mouth. What was he getting at, though? Good God! And why did I go writing all those letters? My own executioner —that's what I am! I can't keep quiet. *I must blab!* And that of all things! I'm heading for destruction, I'm like a boot-rag, and yet I've got to bring my pride into it. "My pride's hurt, I must save it!" I'm my own executioner!'

Thus spoke Mr. Golyadkin, sitting on his ottoman and too frightened to stir. Suddenly his eyes lighted upon an object that excited all his attention. Dreading that it might prove an illusion or figment of his imagination, he reached out his hand timidly, hopefully and with unutterable curiosity towards it. No! It was no illusion, no figment of the imagination. It was without a single shadow of doubt a letter, and it was addressed to him. He picked it up from the table. His heart was pounding within him.

'That scoundrel must have brought it, put it down here, and forgotten about it,' he thought. 'That's probably what happened. That's it.'

The letter was from Vakhrameyev, a young colleague who at one time had been a friend of his.

'Still, I anticipated all this,' thought our hero. 'And I've anticipated what it'll say.'

The letter was as follows:

Dear Yakov Petrovich,

Your man is drunk, and as no sense is to be got from him I prefer to reply by letter. I hasten to inform you that I shall carry out faithfully and exactly the commission you have laid upon me, namely of handing a letter to you know who. This person, who has taken the place of a friend to me—I refrain from mentioning his name, not wishing to sully needlessly the reputation of one who is completely innocent—lodges with us at Karolina Ivanovna's in the room which, when you were staying here, was occupied by an infantry officer from Tambov. He is, however, always to be seen in the company of sincere and honest folk, which is more than I can say for some. I intend to sever my connexions with you as from today, it being impossible for us to preserve the same friendly spirit and unanimity of our former association. And therefore I request, sir, that you forward me on receipt of this candid epistle, the two roubles owing for razors of foreign manufacture which, if you remember, I sold to you on credit seven months ago when you were living with us under the roof of Karolina Ivanovna, a lady for whom I have a most profound respect. I am acting thus because according to accounts I have received from people of intelligence, you have lost your reputation and sense of honour, and become a moral menace to the innocent and uncontaminated. For there are some who abide not by the truth; their words are a lie, and their air of good intent is suspect.

As to standing up for Karolina Ivanovna—who has always been an honourable lady, decorous in demeanour, and who, albeit a spinster no longer in the bloom of youth, is the daughter of a good foreign house—people capable of so doing can always be found everywhere. This I have been asked by several persons to mention to you here in passing, and I do so also on my own behalf. In any case you will learn all in good time, if you have not done so already, for you have by all accounts been making yourself notorious from one end of the capital to the other, and may consequently have heard what you should hear about yourself in many quarters. In conclusion, sir, I must tell you that the person you know, whose name I do not for certain honourable reasons mention—is highly esteemed by right-minded people, and is moreover of a pleasant and cheerful disposition, as successful at his work as he is in intelligent society, and true to his word and to his friends, not insulting them behind their backs while being nice to their faces.

At all events I remain,

Your obedient servant,

N. Vakhrameyev.

PS. Get rid of your man—he is a drunkard and probably causes you a lot of trouble—and take on Yevstafy, who used to be in service here and is now without a place. Your present servant is not only a drunkard but a thief as well. Only last week he sold Karolina Ivanovna a pound of lump sugar on the cheap, which in my opinion he could only have done by steadily stealing small quantities from you over a period. I tell you this as a well-wisher, although all some individuals can do is to insult and deceive everybody, preferably those who are honest and good-natured, slandering them behind their backs, and making them out to be the opposite of what they are, out of pure envy and because they're not as good themselves.

V.

After reading Vakhrameyev's letter, our hero remained motionless on the ottoman for a long while. Some new light was breaking through the vague mysterious mist that had been surrounding him for the past two days. He was beginning to understand a little . . . He was about to try and get to his feet and take a turn or two up and down to refresh himself, collect his scattered thoughts, focus them on a certain subject, and then, having got himself straight a bit, to give the position his mature consideration. But no sooner did he attempt to stand, than he at once fell back again, weak and feeble.

'I anticipated all this, of course. But how did he come to write that, and what do those words really mean? Suppose I do know their sense, where does that lead? He should have told me straight, "Such and such, and such and such, and this and that is required," and I'd have done it. The thing has taken such an unpleasant turn! I wish tomorrow would hurry up and come, and then I could get down to it! I know what to do. "Such and such a thing," I'll say. "I agree to argue it, but I won't sell my honour, etc." But how' this person we know of . . . How's this beastly individual come to get mixed up in it? Why, exactly? Oh, I wish it would soon be tomorrow! Till then they'll slander me! They're intriguing, they're working to spite me! The main thing is not to waste any time, and to write a letter now simply mentioning this and that, and just saying I agree to such and such. And tomorrow at the crack of dawn I'll send it off, then get to the office as early as possible myself, before they do, and forestall these pleasant gentlemen . . . They'll slander me, they will!'

Mr. Golyadkin drew some paper towards him, took pen, and wrote the following reply to Vakhrameyev's letter:

Dear Nestor Ignatyevich,

I have read your obnoxious letter with sorrow and amazement, for I clearly perceive that in speaking of certain indelicate persons and others of false good intent, you are referring to myself. With genuine distress I perceive with what rapidity and success and to what great depths has calumny spread its roots to the detriment of my prosperity, honour and good name. And what is all the more deplorable and outrageous, is that even decent men, genuinely high-minded, and, what is most important, endowed with open, forthright natures, should abandon the interests of honourable folk and attach themselves and all their best qualities to that pernicious putridity which has, unfortunately, been so widely and so very insidiously propagated in our own difficult and unprincipled time. Let me say in conclusion that I shall consider it my sacred duty to repay in full the debt of two roubles that you mention.

Your allusions to a certain female, as also to the intentions, speculations, and various designs of same, I do not, let me tell you, sir, clearly or fully apprehend. I must beg you, sir, to allow me to preserve my high thoughts and good name unsullied. At all events I shall be pleased to enter into explanations with you in person, preferring personal contact to correspondence as being more trustworthy, and am moreover ready to make various peaceable agreements, on mutual terms of course. To this end, sir, I beg that you will intimate to this person my readiness to come to a personal understanding, and request her furthermore to name time and place for the interview. Your insinuations about my having offended you, betrayed our original friendship and spoken slightingly of you, made bitter reading. The whole of this I attribute to misunderstanding, base calumny, and the envy and malevolence of those whom I may justly call my bitterest enemies. They are probably unaware, however, that innocence is the strength of innocence, that their brazen impudence and infuriating familiarity will sooner or later earn them common contempt, and that they will come to destruction solely through their own impropriety and depravity. In conclusion, I beg that you will convey to these persons that their strange pretensions, and their ignoble and chimerical desire to oust others from the places that they occupy by their very existence in the world, and to supplant them, are deserving of consternation, contempt and pity, and what is more, qualify them for the madhouse. Moreover, attitudes such as these are strictly forbidden by law, and in my opinion, quite justly so. There are limits to everything, and if this is a joke, it is a pretty poor one. I will say more—it is utterly immoral, for I venture to assure you, sir, that my own ideas about keeping *one's place,* and these I have amplified above, are purely moral.

I have the honour to remain, Sir,
Your obedient servant,
Y. Golyadkin.

## 10

Mr. Golyadkin had been shaken to the core by the events of the preceding day. He passed an extremely bad night, being unable to get a full five minutes' sleep. It was as if some mischievous person had sprinkled his bed with bristles. He spent the whole time in a semi-somnolent condition, tossing from one side to another, sighing and groaning, dropping off one moment and waking the next; and all this was attended by a strange feeling of anguish, vague memories, hideous visions—in short, by every conceivable unpleasantness.

Sometimes he saw the figure of Andrey Filippovich in a weird mysterious twilight, a gaunt angry figure, with a cold harsh look on its face and some stonily polite word of reprimand on its lips; he would be on the point of going up to Andrey Filippovich to justify himself in some way, and prove that he was not as his enemies made him out to be, but like this and like that, with such and such, and such and such in his favour, over and above his usual innate qualities; but the moment he did so, a certain notoriously beastly person appeared, ruined everything at a single blow and by the most infuriating means, blackened Mr.

Golyadkin's reputation there and then, practically to his face, trampled his pride in the mire, and immediately supplanted him, both at the office and in society.

Sometimes he felt his head tingling from a blow that he had recently received and meekly accepted, either in the society of his fellow men or while performing his duties, when remonstration would have been difficult. As he racked his brains to discover *why* it should have been difficult, his thoughts on this subject would without his noticing it run over into others concerning a certain small but also rather important act of meanness that he had recently witnessed, heard about, or had himself committed, and committed often not for any mean motive or through any mean impulses; sometimes, for instance, it had just been by chance—for reasons of delicacy; another time—because he was completely defenceless; and lastly because . . . But Mr. Golyadkin knew perfectly well *what* it was because of. At this point he would blush in his sleep, and as he tried to hide his blushes, would mutter that there, for instance, one might have shown resolution, a great deal of resolution; and then concluded by asking what that was, and why he need mention it then. But what enraged and exasperated him most of all was that a certain person notorious for his revolting behaviour and scurrilous tendencies would at that moment, whether bidden

or not, unfailingly appear, and with a nasty little
smile mutter quite gratuitously, 'Resolution?
What's that got to do with it? What resolution
could you and I show, Yakov Petrovich?'

Sometimes he would dream that he was in the
splendid company of people celebrated for their
breeding and wit. He, too, distinguished himself
by his amiability and wit, and everyone took a
liking to him—even certain of his enemies who
were present—and this pleased him greatly.
Everyone gave him precedence, and at last he
had the agreeable experience of overhearing the
host speak flatteringly of him to one of the guests
whom he had drawn aside. And all of a sudden,
for no apparent reason, a person notorious for
his evil intentions and brutish impulses in the
shape of Golyadkin junior appeared, and by so
doing demolished at one fell swoop all the glory
and triumph of Golyadkin senior, eclipsing him,
dragging him into the mire and clearly demon-
strating that Golyadkin senior, the real Mr.
Golyadkin, was not real at all but a fraud; *he* was
the real one, and Golyadkin senior was not what
he seemed, but this and that, and consequently
had no right to the society of well-intentioned,
well-bred people. And all this happened so
quickly that Golyadkin senior did not even have
time to open his mouth, before everyone was heart
and soul with the revolting and false Golyadkin
junior, disowning Golyadkin senior, real and

innocent as he was, in a most profoundly con-
temptuous manner. There was no one whose
opinion had not in a twinkling been changed by
the revolting Golyadkin to suit his own. There
was no one, even amongst the lowliest of the
company, on whom the spurious and good-for-
nothing Golyadkin had not fawned in his most
sugary manner—no one with whom he had not
ingratiated himself, and over whom he had not
poured sweet unction that brought tears of delight
to their eyes. And the main thing was that it
all happened in a matter of seconds. The speed
with which the suspect and worthless Golyadkin
moved was astonishing. No sooner had he got
one well-disposed towards him, than before you
could blink, he was quietly making up to another.
The moment he had drawn a benevolent smile
from this one, he jerked his rather dumpy little
legs into life, and was off wooing a third. Before
you had time to register surprise, he was at the
same game with a fourth. It was horrible. It
was sheer wizardry. Everyone was pleased with
him, everyone liked him, everyone praised him
to the skies and proclaimed in chorus that for
amiability and satirical humour he was far and
away above the real Golyadkin, so putting the
latter to shame. They disowned and pushed out
the upright and well-intentioned Golyadkin, and
showered insults upon him who was well-known
for the love he bore his neighbour.

Anguished, terrified and enraged, the Mr. Golyadkin who had suffered so much, rushed out into the street, and tried to hire a cab to take him straight to his Excellency's, or failing that, at least to Andrey Filippovich's. But horror of horrors! The drivers flatly refused him, saying, 'We can't take two people exactly alike, sir. A good man tries hard to live honourably, not just anyhow, and never has a double.'

Looking about him, distracted with shame, the entirely honourable Mr. Golyadkin saw that the cabmen and Petrushka, who had thrown in his lot with them, were right. The depraved Golyadkin was actually standing close beside him, and in his usual blackguardly fashion was at that critical moment preparing to do something very improper that would in no way display the nobility of character acquired by breeding that he, the abominable Golyadkin II, was so fond of vaunting on every suitable occasion.

Out of his mind with shame and despair, the ruined but rightful Mr. Golyadkin fled blindly wherever fate might lead. But as often as his footfalls rang upon the granite pavement, an exact image of Golyadkin the depraved and abominable, would spring up out of the ground. And each of these exact images would come waddling along behind the next, in a long procession like a gaggle of geese, after Golyadkin senior. Escape was impossible. The pitiable Golyadkin grew breathless with terror. In the end there sprang up so fearful a multitude of exact images that the whole capital was blocked with them, and a police officer, perceiving this breach of decorum, was obliged to grab the lot by the scruff of the neck and fling them into a police-box that happened to be near at hand . . .

Our hero awoke, stark frozen with horror. And stark frozen with horror, he realized that his waking hours were hardly any better. He felt tormented and oppressed. His anguish was such that his heart felt as if it were being gnawed from his breast.

Finally he could bear it no longer. 'It shall not be!' he cried, boldly sitting up in bed, and at once came to.

Evidently it had been day for some time. The room was unusually light. Rich sunlight was filtering through the frost-encrusted panes and flooding the walls, which surprised him not a little for this normally happened only at noon, and there had been, to the best of his recollection, no such anomaly in the course of the heavenly luminary before. No sooner had he registered surprise at this, than the wall-clock behind the partition began to make a whirring sound preparatory to striking.

'There!' thought Mr. Golyadkin, and listened anxiously . . .

But the clock, to his final and utter consternation, summoned all its energy, and struck once.

'What's this?' cried our hero, leaping out of bed. Clad as he was, he dashed round the partition, unable to believe his ears. The clock really did say one. He looked at Petrushka's bed, but there was no sign of Petrushka there or anywhere else. The bed had clearly been made for some time and left, and Petrushka's boots were nowhere to be seen—a sure indication that he really was out. Mr. Golyadkin rushed to the door. It was shut.

'Where is he?' he whispered, strangely agitated and feeling his whole body trembling violently. Struck by a sudden thought, he charged to his table, and searched and rummaged about. But Vakhrameyev's letter was gone. Petrushka was gone, the clock said one, and several new points about Vakhrameyev's letter which had been obscure the day before, now became quite clear. At last it was obvious—even Petrushka had been bought! Yes, that was it!

'So that's where the main plot has been hatched!' cried Mr. Golyadkin, striking his forehead, with a look of growing amazement on his face. 'In the den of that odious German woman—that's where the whole evil genius is hidden now! Telling me to go to the Izmaylovsky Bridge was only a strategic diversion. She was putting me off the scent, throwing dust in my eyes—the wicked old hag! That's how she's been undermining me! That's it! If you look at it that way, that's the whole thing exactly—and it accounts for that scoundrel turning up. It all boils down to the same thing. They've been keeping him for a long time, preparing him and saving him up for the fatal day. And see now how it's all turned out—what it's all come to! Ah well, it doesn't matter. No time has been lost!'

Here Mr. Golyadkin remembered with horror that it was now after one.

'What if they've now had time . . .' He uttered a groan. 'No. They won't have. They're telling lies. We'll see . . .'

He flung on some clothes, and seizing pen and paper scribbled the following:

Dear Yakov Petrovich,

It's either you or me. There isn't room for both of us. And therefore I tell you plainly that your strange, ridiculous and unattainable desire to appear my twin and to pass yourself off as such, will serve to achieve nothing more than your complete disgrace and discomfiture. Thus for your own good I must ask you to step down, and make way for those who are genuinely noble and well-intentioned. Failing this, I am prepared to decide in favour of most extreme measures. I lay down my pen, and wait . . .

I remain ready to oblige—even with pistols.

Y. Golyadkin.

When he had finished this note, our hero rubbed his hands vigorously. Then, donning his hat and overcoat, he unlocked the door with a spare key, and set off for the office. But when he got there, he could not make up his mind to go in. It was too late. His watch showed half past two. Suddenly an apparently trivial thing occurred to relieve him of some of his doubts. Around the corner of the office building popped a small, breathless, red-faced figure of a man, who scuttled in a furtive rat-like manner up the steps and into the vestibule. It was Ostafyev, a clerk, who was quite well known to Mr. Golyadkin. He was a useful fellow who would do anything for ten kopeks. Knowing Ostafyev's weakness, and suspecting that after absenting himself from the office 'on some most urgent business', he would be more avid for kopeks than before, our hero made up his mind to be lavish, and slipping up the steps after him, called to him, and with an air of mystery, motioned him into a secluded corner behind an enormous iron stove. Here he began interrogating him.

'Well, my friend, how are things—if you take my meaning?'

'How do you do, sir. At your service, I'm sure.'

'All right, all right, my friend. I'll make it worth your while. Look—how is it?'

'What's that you want to know?' For a moment Ostafyev held his hand up to his mouth which had unexpectedly dropped open.

'Look my friend, I, er . . . Don't go thinking anything— Is Andrey Filippovich here?'

'He is.'

'And the clerks?'

'Here as they should be.'

'And his Excellency as well?'

'And his Excellency as well.' Here the clerk again held his hand up to his gaping mouth, and gave Mr. Golyadkin, or so it seemed, a strangely inquisitive look.

'And there's nothing special, my friend?'

'No, nothing.'

'About me, I mean . . . Isn't there anything . . . You take my meaning?'

'No, nothing at the moment.' The clerk again covered his mouth and looked strangely at Mr. Golyadkin. The latter was now trying to fathom Ostafyev's expression, and discover whether he was keeping anything back. It seemed in fact that he was. He had grown more and more discourteous and unfriendly, and was no longer showing the same sympathetic interest in Mr. Golyadkin's affairs as at the beginning of the conversation.

'He's partly within his rights,' thought Mr. Golyadkin. 'What am I to him? Perhaps the other side has given him something, and that's why he was off "on urgent business". Ah well, I'll um . . .'

He realised the time for disbursing kopeks had come.

'Here you are, my dear chap.'

'Very much obliged, sir.'

'I'll give you more.'

'Yes sir?'

'I'll give you more in a minute, and as much again when we're finished, understand?'

The clerk said nothing, but stood stiff as a ramrod, staring fixedly at him.

'Tell me now, have you heard anything about me?'

'I don't think so . . . Not so far . . .' replied Ostafyev, pausing as he spoke, and maintaining, like Mr. Golyadkin, an air of mystery, wrinkling his brow a little and staring at the floor—in short, doing his utmost to earn what he had been promised. The money he had been given he regarded as earned already.

'Isn't there anything?'

'Not so far.'

'But listen—there may be something, eh?'

'Yes, there may of course.'

'Not so good!' thought our hero.

'Listen, here's something else for you, old fellow.'

'Much obliged, sir, I'm sure.'

'Was Vakhrameyev here yesterday?'

'He was, sir.'

'And anyone else? See if you can remember, old chap.'

The clerk searched his memory for a minute, but could find nothing suitable.

'No sir, no one.'

'Hm!'

A silence followed.

'Look, here's something else for you, my friend. Now tell me all the ins and outs of it.'

'Very good, sir.'

Ostafyev was now as meek as a lamb, which was just what Mr. Golyadkin wanted.

'Tell me old chap, how does he stand now?'

'All right, quite well,' answered the clerk, staring hard at him.

'How well?'

'Well, um . . .' Ostafyev twitched his brows significantly. But he had finally come to a dead end and didn't know what to say.

'It's bad,' thought Mr. Golyadkin.

'Wasn't there some further development with Vakhrameyev?'

'Everything's as it was.'

'Try to think.'

'They say . . .'

'Well?'

Ostafyev put his hand in front of his mouth for a moment.

'Wasn't there a letter for me from there?'

'Mikheyev the caretaker has been to Vakhrameyev's lodgings today—to that German lady there—so I'll go and ask if you like.'

'If you would, my dear chap. Please do, for God's sake. I'm just . . . Don't go thinking anything—I'm just—you know. You inquire and find out whether they're cooking up anything to do with me—what action *he's* taking—that's what I want. You find that out my friend, and I'll make it worth your while.'

'I will sir—and Ivan Semyonych sat in your place today.'

'Ah! He did, did he?'

'Andrey Filippovich told him to.'

'He did? What for? Find that out, my friend. For God's sake find that out! You do all that, and I'll make it up to you, my dear chap. That's what I want to know. And don't you go thinking anything.'

'Very good sir. I'll go at once. Won't you be coming in today?'

'No. I, er . . . I just, um . . . I just came to have a look—but I'll make it worth your while after.'

'All right.'

The clerk ran quickly and eagerly up the stairs, and Mr. Golyadkin was left to himself.

'It's bad,' he thought. 'Bad, bad! Things don't look too good for me. What was the meaning of it all? What did that drunkard mean by some of his hints? Who's at the back of this? Ah! Now I know. They probably found out, and then put him there . . . But did they? It was Andrey

Filippovich put Ivan Semyonovich there. But
why did he do that? What was the point? Very
likely they found out . . . This is Vakhrameyev's
work—no, not Vakhrameyev—he's as stupid as
they make 'em. They're all doing the work for
him. They put that other scoundrel up to coming
here for the same thing. And that one-eyed
German woman made her complaint! I always
suspected all this intrigue had more in it than
met the eye, and that there was bound to be
something in all that old wives' gossip. I said as
much to Dr. Rutenspitz. "They've sworn to cut
someone's throat, in the moral sense," I said "—
and they've got hold of Karolina Ivanovna." No.
This is the work of master hands, you can see
that. It's not Vakhrameyev. No sir, this is the
work of a master! Vakhrameyev's stupid, as I
said . . . But I know now who's doing their
work for them—it's that impostor! That's the
foundation of his career, and that explains why
he's successful in better society. But really I'd
like to know how he stands with them now.
Only *why* have they taken on Ivan Semyonovich?
What damned use is *he* to them? It's as if they
couldn't find anyone else. Still, whoever they
put there it would have been the same. All I
know is, this Ivan Semyonovich has been on my
list of suspects for a long time. I remarked what
a nasty horrible old man he was ages ago. Lends
out money on interest, they say—like a Jew. All

this is the Bear's handiwork. He's been mixed
up in the whole thing. At the Izmaylovsky
Bridge—that's where it all started . . .'

Here Mr. Golyadkin screwed up his face as if
he had bitten a lemon. Evidently he had remembered something very unpleasant.

'Still, it doesn't matter,' he thought. 'It's just
that I keep coming back to my own troubles.
Why doesn't Ostafyev come? He's probably sat
down to something, or been detained somehow.
It's good to have this intrigue afoot and be doing
some undermining of my own. I only have to
give Ostafyev ten kopeks and he's on my side.
But is he? That's the thing! Maybe they've got
at him too, and he's agreed to be part of *their* plot.
He looks a thorough crook! He's keeping something back, the scoundrel! "No, nothing," he
says. "Very much obliged to you sir, I'm sure,"
he says. Cutthroat that he is!'

Hearing a sudden noise, Mr. Golyadkin cowered
back behind the stove. Someone came down the
stairs, and passed out into the street.

'Who could that have been now?' thought our
hero to himself. A minute later other footsteps
were heard. Unable to bear the suspense, he
popped just the tip of his nose out of cover, and
instantly drew it back as if it had been jabbed
with a pin. This time it was someone he knew.
It was the scoundrel, the intriguer, the pervert—
flouncing past with his usual quick horrible little

steps, and throwing out his feet as if he was getting ready to give someone a kick.

'Blackguard,' muttered our hero to himself, but he could not help noticing that the black-guard had under his arm an enormous green dispatch-case belonging to his Excellency.

'Another special errand,' he thought, flushing with vexation and shrinking back still further. No sooner had Golyadkin junior flashed past, unaware of the presence of Golyadkin senior, than a third lot of footsteps were heard, which the latter guessed to be those of the returning clerk. And a clerk it was, a sleek-haired clerk—not Ostafyev, but one Pisarenko—who peered round the stove at Mr. Golyadkin. The latter was amazed.

'Why has he let others into the secret?' he thought. 'Nothing is sacred to this barbarous lot!'

'Well?' he said, turning to Pisarenko. 'Who sent you, my friend?'

'I've come about your business. There's nothing from anyone so far. But if there is, we'll let you know.'

'What about Ostafyev?'

'Couldn't get away. His Excellency's walked through the section twice already, and I can't stay now.'

'Thanks, old man. But tell me . . .'

'Really, I can't stay . . . He's asking for us every

minute . . . You just stand here for a bit, and if there's anything about your business we'll let you know.'

'No, tell me, my friend . . .'

'Please! I can't stay,' said Pisarenko breaking away from Mr. Golyadkin, who had seized him by a lapel. 'Truly, I haven't time. You stand here for a bit and we'll let you know.'

'Just a minute! Just a minute! Look, here's a letter. I'll make it worth your while.'

'All right.'

'Try and give it to Mr. Golyadkin.'

'Golyadkin?'

'Yes, Mr. Golyadkin.'

'All right. As soon as I get off, I'll take it. You stay here meanwhile. No one will see you here.'

'No. Don't go thinking I'm standing here so as not to be seen. I won't be here, I'll be in the side street. There's a coffee-house—that's where I'll be waiting. If anything happens, you'll let me know everything—is that understood?'

'All right. But let me go. I understand.'

'And I'll make it worth your while, old man!' he shouted after Pisarenko, who had at last succeeded in freeing himself.

'That rogue seemed to get ruder towards the end,' thought our hero, creeping out from behind the stove.

'He's another twister—that's clear. First it was this and that . . . Still, he really was in a hurry.

There may be a lot of work. And his Excellency walked through the section twice . . . What was that for? Ah well, it doesn't matter! It may be nothing. We'll see.'

He was about to open the door and go, when at that very moment his Excellency's carriage came thundering up to the entrance. Before he could recover, the occupant had opened the door, and jumped down. It was none other than Golyadkin junior, who had gone out ten minutes before. Golyadkin senior suddenly remembered that the Director's apartments were only a step or two away.

'He's on his special errand,' he thought.

After removing the fat green dispatch-case and some papers from the carriage, and giving some orders to the driver, Golyadkin junior flung open the door, nearly hitting our Mr. Golyadkin, and cutting him dead to spite him, shot up the office stairs.

'It's awful,' thought our hero. 'This is what we've come to now. Heavens above, just look at him!'

For about half a minute our hero stood motionless. At last he made up his mind. Without waiting to think, his heart pounding, and trembling all over, he charged upstairs after his friend.

'Here goes, and I don't care what happens. I'm out of it all,' he thought, as he removed his hat, overcoat and galoshes in the ante-room.

It was nearly dark as Mr. Golyadkin walked into his section. Neither Andrey Filippovich nor Anton Antonovich was there. Both were with the Director handing in their reports, and the Director, as could be plainly heard, was in a hurry to report to a still more exalted person. Because of this, and also because darkness was falling and office hours were drawing to a close, certain clerks, the senior ones mainly, were, at the moment of Mr. Golyadkin's entry, engaged in whiling away the time. They were gathered together talking and laughing, while some of the most junior, the lowest of the low among the clerks, were taking advantage of the general hubbub to have a quiet game of pitch and toss in a corner by the window. Knowing what was proper, and feeling at that moment a particular need to find and win favour, Mr. Golyadkin went up to some of those he knew best to pass the time of day and so forth. But his colleagues reacted somewhat strangely to his greetings. He was unpleasantly struck by a certain iciness, abruptness, and one might almost say sternness, in the way they received him. No one held out a hand. Some simply said hello and walked away; some merely nodded; one turned his back, pretending not to have noticed him; while others—and this is what was more offensive to Mr. Golyadkin than anything else—others, that is to say some of the most junior ungraded clerks, mere lads, who, as he had rightly said, were only good for playing pitch and toss and roaming the streets, gradually surrounded him in such a way as to make escape almost impossible. They all looked at him with a sort of impudent curiosity.

It was an ill omen. He sensed that, and wisely prepared to ignore it. Then all of a sudden something quite unexpected happened, that finished— that completely sank him, as the saying is.

Suddenly, almost as if on purpose, at what was his most anxious moment, Golyadkin junior appeared among the encircling clerks. Gay, smiling, full of beans as ever, nimble-footed, nimble-tongued, he frolicked, toadied, gambolled and guffawed. He was, in short, his usual self— exactly as he had been the day before, when he had also turned up at a most unpleasant moment for Mr. Golyadkin.

Skipping, simpering and whirling around with a smile that wished 'Good evening' to all assembled, he burst in on the little crowd of clerks. One he shook by the hand, another he clapped on the shoulder, a third he lightly embraced, to a fourth he explained the business on which he had been employed by his Excellency—where he had been, what he had done, and what he had taken with him—and a fifth, who was probably his best friend, he kissed resoundingly on the lips . . . To put it briefly, everything was happening just as in Golyadkin senior's dream.

When he had capered about to his heart's

content, when he had dealt with them all in his own inimitable way, disposing each and every one of them favourably towards himself, whether there was any need or not, suddenly and probably in error, having so far failed to notice his oldest friend, Golyadkin junior even stretched out his hand to Golyadkin senior. The latter, probably also in error, although he had had ample time to observe the ignoble Golyadkin junior, eagerly seized the unexpectedly proffered hand, and impelled by some sudden strange inner urge, tearfully grasped it in the firmest and friendliest manner. Whether he had been deceived by his enemy's first move, whether he had lost his presence of mind or sensed and realized in his heart of hearts how completely defenceless he was, is difficult to say. The fact remains that Golyadkin senior, in full possession of his faculties, of his own free will and before witnesses, solemnly shook the hand of him he called his mortal foe. But how great his amazement and fury, horror and shame, when his foe and mortal enemy, perceiving the error of the innocent man he had persecuted and perfidiously deceived, suddenly, with insufferable effrontery and grossness, brazenly, callously, and showing neither conscience nor compassion, snatched his hand away! Not satisfied with that, he shook it as if it had been contaminated. Even worse, he spat, and made a most offensive gesture! And worst of all, taking

out his handkerchief, he wiped each finger that
had momentarily rested in the hand of Golyadkin
senior. All the while he looked about him
deliberately, in his usual blackguardly way, so that
all should see what he was doing, and looked
everyone in the face in an obvious attempt to
convey to them most unpleasant things about
Golyadkin senior. The behaviour of the odious
Golyadkin junior seemed to arouse general indignation amongst the encircling clerks. Even the
empty-headed juniors indicated their disapproval.
There were murmurs on all sides. The general
stir did not fail to impress itself on Golyadkin
senior, but a sudden well-timed sally from Golyadkin junior shattered and destroyed our hero's
last hopes, and restored the balance in favour or
his deadly foe.

'Our Russian Faublas, gentlemen! Allow me
to present the young Faublas,' squeaked Golyadkin
junior with his customary insolence, rapidly weav-
ing his way through the clerks and pointing at the
petrified but genuine Mr. Golyadkin.

'Let us embrace, my dear fellow!' he continued
with unbearable familiarity, making towards the
man he had treacherously insulted. The worthless Golyadkin junior's sally found a ready response, containing as it did a cunning allusion with
which all were evidently familiar. Our hero felt
the hand of his enemies heavy upon him. But
his mind was finally made up. With eyes ablaze

and a rigid smile upon his pallid face, he somehow
broke out of the crowd, and with uneven hurried
steps made straight for his Excellency's sanctum.
With one room to go, he met Andrey Filippovich
just returning from his Excellency's presence, and
although there were quite a number of people
about who were at that moment strangers to Mr.
Golyadkin, he tried not to pay any attention to
them. Boldly, openly and resolutely, amazed by
his own temerity and yet inwardly praising himself for it, he accosted Andrey Filippovich on the
spot. The latter was very much taken aback by
this unexpected assault.

'Ah! What do you, er ... What do you want?'
asked the departmental head, not listening to what
Mr. Golyadkin was trying to stutter.

'Andrey Filippovich . . . Andrey Filippovich,
can I talk to his Excellency confidentially?' asked
our hero clearly and distinctly, giving Andrey
Filippovich one of his most determined looks.

'What? Of course not.' Andrey Filippovich
looked Mr. Golyadkin up and down.

'I say all this, Andrey Filippovich, because I am
amazed that no one here should have unmasked
this rogue and impostor.'

'Wha-at?'

'This impostor . . .'

'Who are you calling that?'

'A certain person, Andrey Filippovich—it's a
certain person I'm getting at. I'm within my

rights. I think our superior ought to encourage such action,' added Mr. Golyadkin, obviously beside himself. 'You can probably see yourself, Andrey Filippovich, that it's acting honourably and that it shows every kind of good intention on my part to regard our superior as a father. I look upon our benevolent superior as a father, and blindly trust him with my fate. That's how it is . . .'

His voice began to tremble, his face grew red, and two tears ran down his eyelashes.

So amazed was Andrey Filippovich by what Mr. Golyadkin had said, that he involuntarily started back a couple of paces. He looked around uneasily. How things would have ended it is difficult to say. But all of a sudden the door of his Excellency's sanctum opened, and his Excellency himself emerged, accompanied by several officials. Everyone in the room followed on after them. His Excellency beckoned Andrey Filippovich and walked beside him, opening conversation on some matter of business. When they had all moved off, Mr. Golyadkin recovered. Now in a quieter state, he took refuge beneath the wing of Anton Antonovich, who came hobbling along last of all, with what seemed a stern and apprehensive look on his face.

'I've let my tongue run away with me, and I've made a mess of it this time too,' he thought to himself. 'Well, it doesn't matter.'

'I hope that you at least will consent to hear me, Anton Antonovich, and consider my case,' he said softly, his voice still trembling a little with emotion.

'Spurned by all, I appeal to you. I'm still wondering what Andrey Filippovich meant by what he said. Please explain to me if you can.'

'It will all be explained in good time,' replied Anton Antonovich severely, and paused with a look that seemed to make it quite clear that he had no desire to continue the conversation. 'You'll soon know all about it. You'll be informed officially today.'

'What do you mean by "officially", Anton Antonovich? Why "officially"?' he inquired timidly.

'It's not for us to discuss what our superiors are deciding, Yakov Petrovich.'

'Our superiors?' said Mr. Golyadkin, growing still more timid. 'Why our superiors? I see no reason for bothering them, Anton Antonovich. Perhaps you mean something about yesterday.'

'No. It's nothing to do with yesterday. This is something else that's wrong with you.'

'"Wrong", Anton Antonovich? I don't think there is.'

'Weren't you going to "fox" somebody?' asked Anton Antonovich, sharply cutting short the perplexed Mr. Golyadkin.

The latter shuddered and went as white as a sheet.

'Of course, Anton Antonovich, if you pay attention to slander, and listen to people's enemies without hearing what the other side has to say, then of course one just has to suffer, innocently and for nothing,' he said in a voice that was barely audible.

'Precisely. And how about your improper behaviour that prejudiced the good name of a noble young lady, of a highly moral, respected and well-known family that had done you a lot of good?'

'What behaviour, Anton Antonovich?'

'Precisely. And the laudable way you've acted towards another lady who, although poorly-off, is of honourable foreign extraction—you don't know anything about that either?'

'Listen, Anton Antonovich—listen to me, please!'

'And your treachery, and slandering of someone else—accusing him of something you're guilty of yourself—what d'you call that, eh?'

'I didn't drive him out, Anton Antonovich,' said our hero, beginning to quake. 'And I didn't put Petrushka—my man that is—up to anything like that either . . . He ate my bread, Anton Antonovich. He enjoyed my hospitality,' added our hero with such expression and deep feeling that his chin began to tremble slightly, and tears were all ready to start to his eyes.

'That's what you say, Yakov Petrovich,' smirked Anton Antonovich, and there was a

note of slyness in his voice that clawed at Mr.
Golyadkin's heart.

'Let me humbly ask you one more thing,
Anton Antonovich. Does his Excellency know
about all this?'

'Of course! But you must let me go now.
I haven't got time to spend with you. You'll hear
all you should today.'

'Please, Anton Antonovich, just one minute
more, for God's sake!'

'You can tell me afterwards.'

'No, Anton Antonovich, you see I . . . Please
just listen . . . I'm no advocate of free-thinking.
I keep away from it. I'm quite prepared myself
—and have on the contrary been known to
say . . .'

'All right, all right. I've heard that.'

'No, Anton Antonovich, you haven't—not
this. This is different, Anton Antonovich. This
is good—really it is. It makes pleasant listening . . .
I have, as I've said before, made it known as my
view that these two identical beings were created
by Providence, and that our beneficent superiors,
seeing the hand of Providence, gave the twins
refuge. That's good, Anton Antonovich—very
good, you can see it is, and you can see I'm far
from being a free-thinker. I look upon our beneficent superior as a father. "Such and such," says
our beneficent superior, "and you, er . . . A
young man must have employment," he says . . .

'Back me up, Anton Antonovich. Take my part. I don't mean anything ... For God's sake, Anton Antonovich, just one more word ... Anton Antonovich!'

But Anton Antonovich was already some distance away. So shaken and bewildered was our hero by all that he had heard and experienced, that he had no idea where he was, what he had been told, or what he had done. He had no idea of what had happened to him, or of what was going to happen.

With an imploring gaze he searched the throng of clerks for Anton Antonovich, intending to justify himself still further in the latter's eyes, and make some extremely reasonable, generous and agreeable remark about himself. But gradually new light was beginning to penetrate his troubled mind, a new and terrible light that suddenly revealed a whole vista of things hitherto quite unknown and totally unsuspected. At that moment our disconcerted hero felt a nudge in his ribs, and looking round saw Pisarenko.

'A letter, sir.'

'Ah! You've been round then, old chap?'

'No. It came here this morning at ten o'clock. Sergey Mikheyevich, the porter, brought it from Vakhrameyev's place.'

'All right, all right old chap. I'll make it up to you.'

So saying, Mr. Golyadkin concealed the letter

in a side-pocket, and buttoned his jacket right up. He then took a look round, and noted to his astonishment that he was in the vestibule, and standing amidst a crowd of clerks who, since office hours were over, had been making for the door. Nor was this last fact the only thing that had escaped his notice, for he had no memory or recollection of how he came suddenly to be wearing his overcoat and galoshes, and holding his hat.

The clerks were all standing stock-still, waiting respectfully. His Excellency had stopped at the bottom of the steps, and while awaiting his carriage, which for some reason was delayed, was having a very interesting conversation with Andrey Filippovich and a couple of counsellors. Somewhat removed from these three, stood Anton Antonovich Setochkin and some other clerks, who, seeing his Excellency laughing and joking, were themselves all smiles. The clerks gathered at the top of the steps were also smiling as they waited for another laugh from his Excellency. The only one who was not smiling was Fedoseich, the corpulent commissionaire who stood, stiff as a ramrod, grasping the handle and waiting impatiently for his diurnal portion of pleasure, which consisted in flinging open one of the doors with a single sweep of his arm, bowing to the ground, and ceremoniously allowing his Excellency to pass. But the one whose pleasure and happiness

seemed greatest of all, was Mr. Golyadkin's unworthy and ignoble enemy. He was for the
moment oblivious of all his colleagues, had even
left off fussing and trotting round them in his
usual odious way, and was even neglecting a
suitable opportunity for making up to someone.
He was all eyes and ears, his gaze did not shift
from his Excellency, and he seemed in some
strange fashion to have shrunk—probably in the
effort to hear better. Only an occasional and
barely perceptible twitch of arm, leg or head
betrayed his secret impulses.

'He's quite giddy with it!' thought our hero.
'He looks the favourite, the scoundrel! I'd like
to know just how he manages to succeed in good
society—no brains, no character, no refinement,
no feeling! He's got luck, the villain. Good God!
When you think of it, how quickly one can get
on, and make friends with everybody. And he'll
get on! He'll go a long way, I swear he will!
He'll get there, he's got luck! Another thing
I'd like to know is what he keeps whispering in
everyone's ear all the time, what mysteries they're
starting between them, and what secrets they talk
about. Oh God! How could I just . . . How
could I get in with them as well? "Such and such,"
I'd say—perhaps I should ask him . . . "Such and
such," I'd tell him, "and I won't do it again. It
was all my fault," I'd say, "but a young man can't
live without work nowadays, your Excellency.

My obscure position doesn't trouble me at all."
That's it! I won't protest in any way. I'll put up
with it all humbly and patiently—that's what I'll
do. But is that really the way to act? No. You'll
never get the scoundrel to see reason—he's too
thick-skinned. You can't hammer any sense into
him—he doesn't give a damn for anything. Still,
we'll have a try. If I happen to hit on a good
moment, I'll try . . .'

Sensing in his anguish, agitation and bewilderment that things could not be left like that,
that the decisive moment was at hand, and that
there was someone he must come to an understanding with, our hero was just moving a little
closer to where his unworthy and enigmatic
friend was standing, when his Excellency's long-
awaited carriage came thundering up to the entrance. Fedoseich flung open the door, and
bowing low, let his Excellency out. All those
who had been waiting at once rushed for the
door, and Golyadkin senior was for the moment
thrust away from Golyadkin junior.

'You won't get away!' thought our hero,
forcing his way forward, and keeping his quarry
in sight. The crowd opened out at last, and suddenly feeling himself free, he charged in pursuit
of his enemy.

## 11

HIS lungs bursting, Mr. Golyadkin sped after his rapidly retiring adversary as if on wings. He felt tremendous energy inside him. But for all his energy he had no doubt that a mere mosquito, had such a creature been able to exist in St. Petersburg at such a time, could easily have knocked him down with one wing. He felt that he had grown utterly weak and feeble, and that he was being borne along not by his own legs —for these were buckling beneath him and no longer obedient—but by some quite peculiar external force. Still, all that might turn out for the best.

'It might, and it might not,' thought our hero, almost stifled for lack of breath after running so hard. 'But the game's up—there isn't a shadow of doubt. I'm sunk—that's certain. The whole thing is signed sealed and delivered.'

All the same, he felt suddenly resurrected—felt as if he had lasted out the battle and snatched a victory, as he succeeded in seizing his enemy's overcoat, just as the latter had one foot on the step of a cab.

'Sir! Sir!' he cried to the ignoble Golyadkin junior—'I trust that you will . . .'

'Please don't then,' replied his callous enemy evasively, one foot on the step, the other waving uselessly in the air, as he strove to get it into the cab, maintain his balance, and at the same time to wrench his coat away from Golyadkin senior, who was clutching it with all the strength nature had bestowed upon him.

'Yakov Petrovich—just ten minutes . . .'

'Excuse me, I haven't time.'

'You must agree, Yakov Petrovich . . . Please, Yakov Petrovich . . . For God's sake, Yakov Petrovich. Let's have it out . . . Man to man . . . One second, Yakov Petrovich!'

'My dear good fellow, I must dash,' replied the other with discourteous familiarity disguised as sincere *bonhomie*. 'Some other time . . . With the best will in the world, believe me . . . I really can't now.'

'Blackguard!' thought our hero. 'Yakov Petrovich!' he cried, filled with anguish, 'I have never been your enemy. Spiteful people have given an unfair picture of me. For my part I'm prepared . . . If you like, let's go somewhere this minute—you and I—shall we, Yakov Petrovich? Let's go into this coffee-house, and with the best will in the world, as you rightly said just now, let's talk it over, nobly, man to man. Everything will explain itself, Yakov Petrovich. It's bound to.'

'This coffee-house? All right, I don't mind.

But on one condition, old chap, and on one condition only, that everything *does* explain itself,' said Golyadkin junior, getting down from the cab and brazenly clapping our hero on the shoulder. 'You're a dear good friend, and for you I'm ready "to take a little side street", as you once put it. You really are a rascal, you do just what you like with a man,' he continued with a smile, coaxing and cajoling him.

The coffee-house into which the two Mr. Golyadkins went, stood secluded from the main streets, and was at that moment quite deserted. No sooner had they sounded the bell, than a plumpish German woman appeared behind the counter. Mr. Golyadkin and his unworthy enemy passed through into a second room, where a pasty-faced urchin with close-cropped hair was fiddling around by the stove with a bundle of firewood, making an effort to bring some life back into a dead fire. At Golyadkin junior's request, chocolate was served.

'There's a nice full-bodied woman,' said Golyadkin junior, with a roguish wink at Golyadkin senior.

Our hero blushed and said nothing.

'But forgive me, I forgot. I know what you fancy. We're sweet on *slim* little Fräuleins you and I, aren't we, Yakov Petrovich? Not-un-attractive, slim little Fräuleins? We lodge with them, we lead them astray, we give them our hearts for their *Biersuppe* and their *Milchsuppe,* we give them various written undertakings—that's what we do, isn't it—you Faublas, you serpent!'

While making these utterly futile albeit fiendishly subtle allusions to a certain person of the female sex, Golyadkin junior had been fawning on Golyadkin senior, and affecting an amiable smile in a false show of affability and pleasure at their meeting. But noticing that Golyadkin senior was by no means so stupid or lacking in education and breeding as immediately to take him at his word, the ignoble man decided to change his tactics and come into the open. With infuriating effrontery and familiarity, the spurious Golyadkin followed up his odious speech by slapping the trustworthy Golyadkin on the back—not content with which, he began to frolic in a manner quite unbecoming in good society, and suddenly took it into his head to repeat his former heinous trick of pinching—regardless of his resistance and subdued cries—the indignant Mr. Golyadkin's cheek. Confronted with such depravity, our hero seethed with rage, and remained silent—but only for a while.

'That is what my enemies say,' he replied finally, prudently keeping himself in check. His voice trembled. Golyadkin junior was evidently in excellent spirits, and ready to indulge in all sorts of pranks inadmissible in a public place, and, generally speaking, in good society.

'Just as you please,' answered Golyadkin junior gravely, draining his cup in a shamefully greedy fashion, and placing it on the table.

'Well, I haven't much time to spend with you. How are you getting on now, Yakov Petrovich?'

'There's only one thing I can say to you, Yakov Petrovich,' replied our hero coolly and with dignity, 'I have never been your enemy.'

'Hm-m . . . Well, how's Petrushka? I think that's his name, isn't it? How is he—all right? Same as ever?'

'The same as ever,' answered Golyadkin senior, a little taken aback. 'I don't know, Yakov Petrovich, but for my part—from a candid and honourable point of view—you'll agree yourself . . .'

'Yes. But you know yourself, Yakov Petrovich, these are hard times we live in,' replied Golyadkin junior quietly and expressively, making himself out to be sorrowful, repentant, and worthy of pity. 'I appeal to you, Yakov Petrovich—you're a clever man and will judge fairly,' he threw in as an abject piece of flattery. 'Life isn't a game—you know yourself,' he concluded, making himself out to be the wise and learned man able to discourse on lofty subjects.

'For my part, Yakov Petrovich,' answered our hero animatedly, 'scorning beating about the bush, speaking honourably, openly, man to man and straight from the shoulder, and putting the whole thing on an honourable level, I tell you,

Yakov Petrovich—I can assert frankly and honourably that I am perfectly blameless, and that, as you know yourself . . . an error on both sides . . . anything is possible . . . the world's judgment, the opinion of the servile throng . . . I tell you frankly, Yakov Petrovich, anything is possible. I'll say more, if one considers the matter thus, if one regards it from a noble and lofty point of view, then I will say boldly, without any false shame, that it will be a pleasure to find I've been mistaken, and a pleasure to admit it. You know yourself—you're intelligent and generous . . . Without shame, without any false shame, I'm ready to admit it . . .' he concluded, nobly and with dignity.

'It's fate, Yakov Petrovich. But let's leave all this,' sighed Golyadkin junior. 'Let us rather employ these brief minutes together in pleasant and profitable conversation, as two colleagues should. Really, all this time I don't seem to have said two words to you. I'm not to blame for that.'

'Nor I!' interrupted our hero eagerly. 'My heart tells me that. Let's blame it all on fate,' he added in a thoroughly conciliatory tone. His voice was gradually beginning to weaken and quaver.

'Well, how are you keeping?' inquired the erring one agreeably.

'Coughing a bit.' answered our hero still more agreeably.

'Look after yourself. With all the epidemics

that are going about, you can easily get throat trouble. I don't mind telling you, I'm starting to wear flannel.'

'Yes. You can easily get throat trouble,' said our hero after a short silence. 'Yakov Petrovich, I see I've been wrong! I'm touched by the memory of those happy moments we passed together beneath my humble, but I venture to say hospitable roof.'

'That's not what you said in your letter,' rejoined Golyadkin junior somewhat reproachfully. And for once he was perfectly right.

'I was wrong, Yakov Petrovich! I now see clearly I was wrong in that unfortunate letter of mine. I feel ashamed to look at you. You can't believe . . . Give me that letter so that I can tear it up in front of your eyes. And if that's not possible, then I beseech you, read it the other way round in a deliberately friendly way, giving each word its reverse meaning. I was wrong. Forgive me, Yakov Petrovich—I've been utterly, grievously wrong.'

'What's that?' inquired Mr. Golyadkin's perfidious friend in an indifferent, absent-minded sort of way.

'I say I've been utterly wrong, Yakov Petrovich, and for my part, I'm completely without false shame . . .'

'Ah well, that's all right then,' retorted Golyadkin junior rudely.

'I even had the idea,' added our hero nobly, completely unaware of the dreadful perfidy of his false friend, 'I even had the idea of two identical beings being created . . .'

'You did?'

At this point the notoriously worthless Golyadkin junior rose, and reached for his hat. Still blind to the hoax, Golyadkin senior rose also, smiling generously and good-naturedly at his false friend, and endeavouring in his innocence to be nice to him, to reassure him, and so to strike up a new friendship.

'Farewell, your Excellency!' cried Golyadkin junior suddenly.

Our hero shuddered, noticing something almost Bacchanalian in his enemy's face, and with the sole object of getting rid of him, thrust two fingers into the reprobate's outstretched hand. But the brazenness of Golyadkin junior exceeded all limits. After first gripping his two fingers, the worthless man decided to repeat before his very eyes the shameless trick he had performed that afternoon. It was more than flesh and blood could stand . . .

He was just pocketing the handkerchief with which he had wiped his fingers, when Mr. Golyadkin recovered his senses, and rushed after him into the next room, whither in his usual noxious way he had hastened to effect his escape. There he was, standing by the counter as if it were the most natural thing in the world, eating pastries and making polite conversation to the German confectioneress—just like any decent moral person.

'Not in front of ladies,' thought our hero, and went up to the counter, almost beside himself in his agitation.

'She's not bad. What do you think?' said Golyadkin junior, up to his smutty pranks again, counting no doubt on Mr. Golyadkin's infinite patience.

The plump German woman looked at both customers with her dull stupid eyes, and smiled affably, obviously not understanding a word of Russian. Our hero flushed fiery red, and unable to control himself, sprang at the shameless man, evidently intending to tear him limb from limb, and finish him for good. But Golyadkin junior was as usual far away—he had taken to his heels and was already out of the door. Needless to say, Golyadkin senior, as soon as he had recovered from the first momentary feeling of bewilderment that had naturally beset him, charged as fast as his legs would carry him in pursuit of his abuser, who was getting into the cab which had obviously been waiting for him by agreement. At that moment however, the plump German, seeing the flight of her two customers, gave a shriek and rang her little bell as hard as she could. Turning almost in mid-air, our hero threw her

some money to cover himself and the shameless
man who had left without paying, and without
waiting for change, succeeded, in spite of this
delay and again almost in mid-air, in catching up
with his enemy. He seized hold of the splash-
board by every means in his power, and was
carried some way along the street, struggling to
clamber onto the carriage, while Golyadkin
junior did his utmost to fight him off. The driver
urged on his sorry horse, using words, whip, reins
and feet, until quite unexpectedly it burst into a
gallop, taking the bit between its teeth and kicking
up its hind legs in a peculiarly nasty fashion. At
last our hero managed to hoist himself up into a
position where he sat back to back with the
driver, and face to face and knee to knee with
his brazen, depraved and most obdurate foe,
gripping the moth-eaten fur collar of the latter's
overcoat in his right hand.

The enemies were carried some way in silence.
Our hero could scarcely recover his breath. The
road was terrible, and he was continually being
thrown into the air and in danger of having his
neck broken, added to which his enemy, still refusing to admit defeat, strove to topple him into
the mud. To crown everything, the weather was
as bad as it could possibly be. Snow fell in huge
flakes which did their best in every way to creep
inside the unbuttoned overcoat of the real Mr.
Golyadkin. All around not a thing could be seen.

It was difficult to tell through what streets and in which direction they were going. It seemed to Mr. Golyadkin that there was something familiar about what was happening to him. For a moment he tried hard to remember whether he had not had some presentiment or other the day before —in a dream for instance. His anguish at last became acute agony. He pressed himself against his pitiless foe, and was about to utter a cry, but it died on his lips.

It was at this moment that Mr. Golyadkin forgot everything, and decided the whole thing didn't matter; it was all just happening in some inexplicable way, and it would be vain and so much wasted effort to protest. But suddenly, almost as he was deciding this, an inconsiderate jolt altered the whole complexion of the matter. He fell from the carriage like a sack of potatoes and rolled over and over, confessing as he did so, and quite rightly, that his fit of temper had really been most inopportune. Jumping to his feet, he saw that the cab had stopped in the middle of a courtyard which he recognised at a glance as that belonging to the house wherein resided Olsufy Ivanovich. The same instant he noticed his enemy mounting the steps, probably on his way to visit Olsufy Ivanovich. In indescribable anguish he was about to rush and catch him up, but fortunately and sensibly thought better of it. Not forgetting first to settle up with the cab-driver, he dashed out into the street and ran on blindly as fast as his legs would carry him.

It was wet, dark and snowing hard, just as before. Our hero did not run, he flew, bouncing off and bowling over men women and children as he went. From all quarters came shrieks, shouts and a fearful hubbub of voices, but Mr. Golyadkin seemed barely conscious, and heeded none of it. He came to by the Semyonovsky Bridge, and then only because he had collided awkwardly with two peasant women, knocking them over together with the goods they were hawking, and falling down himself.

'It doesn't matter,' he thought, 'it can all be settled for the best,' and immediately slipped his hand into his pocket for a rouble to make good the gingerbreads, apples, peas and various other things he had upset. Suddenly new light dawned upon him; in his pocket he felt the letter he had been handed that afternoon. Remembering there was an inn he knew close by, he ran off to it, and once inside, lost no time in establishing himself at a small table lit by a tallow candle. Heedless of all around, and ignoring the waiter who appeared for his order, he broke the seal, and began to read the following, which utterly amazed him:

To the noble one who suffers for my sake and is eternally dear to my heart.

I am in distress, I perish, save me! A slanderer,

intriguer and notoriously worthless man has en-
snared me and I am undone, lost! Him I abominate, while you . . . We have been kept apart, my
letters to you have been intercepted, and all this
has been done by an immoral man availing himself
of his one and only good quality—his likeness to
you. One can however be ugly, but still fascinate
by one's wit, strong sensibilities and good manners . . .

I perish! I am being forcibly married, and the one
who has schemed most in this, desiring probably
to secure my place and connexions in good society,
is my father, my benefactor, the Civil Counsellor
Olsufy Ivanovich. But my mind is made up, and
I protest by every means in my power. Await me
in your carriage outside Olsufy Ivanovich's windows
tonight at nine exactly. We are having another
ball, and the handsome lieutenant is coming. I
shall leave, and we shall fly.

Besides, there are other official posts where one
may still be of service to one's country. Remember at all events, my friend, that innocence is the
strength of innocence.

Farewell. Be waiting with the carriage at the
entrance. I shall rush to your protecting embrace
at 2 a.m. precisely.

Yours till the grave,<br>Klara Olsufyevna.

For some minutes he remained thunderstruck.

Then, in a fearful state of anguish and agitation, and with his face as white as a sheet, he paced several times up and down the room, holding the letter in his hand. To complete the awfulness of his situation, although he was not at that moment aware of it, every eye in the place was upon him. His disordered clothes, his lack of control, his walking, or rather dashing up and down the room, his two-handed gesticulations and the few enigmatic words he addressed absent-mindedly to the world at large, all this can have done little to commend him to the other customers. Even the waiter began to look at him suspiciously. Recovering his senses, our hero found himself standing in the middle of the room, and staring in a rude and almost shameless way at a very respectable-looking old man who, having finished dinner and offered thanks before an ikon, had resumed his seat, and was staring back. Our hero looked about him uneasily, and saw everyone looking at him in a most ominous and suspicious fashion. Suddenly a retired army man with a red collar to his tunic called loudly for *The Police Gazette*. Mr. Golyadkin shuddered, blushed, and chancing to look down suddenly, noticed that his attire was unseemly to a degree that would have been inadmissible in his own home, let alone in a public place. His boots, trousers and the whole of his left side were plastered in mud. His left trouser-strap had been ripped off, and his coat was torn in many places. In sore distress, he went over to the table at which he had been reading, and saw the waiter approaching with a strange, impudently insistent look on his face. Bewildered and utterly dejected, Mr. Golyadkin began to examine the table at which he was standing. There were plates left from somebody's dinner, a dirty serviette, and a recently-discarded knife, fork and spoon.

'Who's been eating here?' he wondered. 'Could it have been me? Anything is possible.'

Looking up, he again saw the waiter standing beside him, and on the point of saying something.

'What do I owe you, old chap?' inquired our hero in a voice that quavered.

There was loud laughter all around. The waiter smiled. Mr. Golyadkin realised he had put his foot in it, and committed some awful blunder. He was so overcome with confusion, that he was constrained to feel for his handkerchief, just for the sake of something to do, instead of simply standing there. But to his indescribable amazement as well as to that of all around, in place of his handkerchief he pulled out the bottle of medicine prescribed by Dr. Rutenspitz four days earlier. 'Get it at the same chemist's,' flashed through his mind. Suddenly he shuddered and almost screamed with terror. New light was dawning. The dark loathsome reddish fluid gleamed ominously before his eyes. The bottle slipped from his grasp and was instantly smashed. With a cry he leapt back to avoid the spilled liquid. He was trembling in every limb. Sweat was breaking out upon his brow and temples.

'So my life is in danger!'

The room was filled with uproar and excitement. They were all surrounding him, they were all saying things to him, some were even laying hold of him. But our hero was speechless, motionless, unseeing, unhearing and unfeeling. At last, tearing himself away, he rushed from the inn, shaking off all and sundry who sought to detain him. He collapsed almost unconscious into the first cab that came along, and hurtled back to his rooms.

On his way in he met Mikheyev the office porter, holding an official envelope in his hand.

'I know, my friend. I know it all, it's official,' said our exhausted hero, weakly and miserably.

The envelope did in fact contain an order signed by Andrey Filippovich to the effect that he should hand over to Ivan Semyonovich. Taking it and giving the porter ten kopeks, Mr. Golyadkin entered his rooms to find Petrushka piling all his belongings and odds and ends together, obviously intending to leave him and go to Karolina Ivanovna, who had enticed him into replacing Yevstafy.

## 12

PETRUSHKA came swinging into Mr. Golyadkin's room. His manner was singularly casual, and he had the menial's look of triumph on his face. He had evidently got some idea into his head, and was feeling quite within his rights. He looked a complete stranger, that is, like someone else's servant, and nothing like the former servant of Mr. Golyadkin.

'I say old fellow,' began our hero, still short of breath, 'what's the time now?'

Without a word Petrushka went behind the partition, and coming back, announced in a rather independent tone of voice that it was nearly seven-thirty.

'Oh, that's fine. Well, if I may say so my dear fellow, everything seems over between us.'

Petrushka said nothing.

'Since it is, tell me frankly now, as you would a friend, where it is you've been.'

'Me?—With nice people.'

'I know, my friend, I know. You've always given me satisfaction, and I'll give you a reference. So you're with them now, are you?'

'Well sir, you know yourself, a good man won't teach you any bad ways, of course.'

'I know, I know old fellow. Good people are rare nowadays. Treasure them, my friend. And how are they?'

'You know how they are, sir. Only I can't work for you any more now, you can see that.'

'I do, I do my dear chap. I know how keen and hard-working you are. I've seen it all, I've noticed. I respect you, my friend. I respect a good honest man, even if he's a servant.'

'Yes, I know. Our sort, of course, as you know yourself, must go where things are best. That's how it is. And what can I do about it? It's well known sir—without a good man, it's impossible.'

'Yes, yes. I appreciate that. Well, here's your money and your reference. Now let's shake hands and say good-bye. There's just one last thing I'd like to ask you to do,' said Mr. Golyadkin solemnly. 'You see my dear chap, anything can happen. Sorrow lurks e'en in gilded halls, my friend, and you can't get away from it. I think I've always been kind to you, you know . . .'

Petrushka said nothing.

'I think I've always been kind to you . . . How am I off for linen, my dear fellow?'

'It's all there. Six shirts linen, three pairs socks, four shirt-fronts, one vest flannel, two sets underwear. You know all that yourself. I've got nothing of yours. I look after my master's things.

You know me, sir. That's never been one of my weaknesses. You know that.'

'I believe you, my friend. I believe you. That's not what I mean. You see . . .'

'I know. We all know that, sir. Why, when I was with General Stolbnyakov—he let me go when he went to Saratov—he had an estate there . . .'

'No, my friend. I don't mean that. I don't mean anything like that. Don't go thinking anything, my dear fellow . . .'

'I know. The likes of us can be slandered any minute, as you're well aware. But I've given satisfaction everywhere. Ministers, generals, senators, counts, I've been with them all. Prince Svinchatkin, Colonel Pereborkin, General Nedobarov—he also went away to his estate . . .'

'Yes my friend, yes. Very good. And now *I'm* going away. We all have different roads to travel, my dear fellow, and no one knows on which he may find himself. Now give me a hand to get dressed. Lay out my uniform jacket, my other trousers, sheets, blankets, pillows . . .'

'Shall I make a bundle of it all?'

'Yes please, my dear fellow. A bundle. Who knows what may happen to us? And now you go and find me a carriage.'

'A carriage?'

'Yes my friend, a big roomy one, and for a definite time. And don't go getting any ideas . . .'

'Do you wish to go far?'

'I don't know, my friend. That's also something I don't know. My feather-bed had better go in too, I think. What do you think, my dear chap? I'm relying on you.'

'Are you actually thinking of going now, sir?'

'I am, my friend. I am. That's how things have turned out. So there it is.'

'I know, sir. Same thing happened to a lieutenant in our regiment. He carried off the daughter of the local landowner.'

'Carried her off? How do you mean, my dear good fellow?'

'Yes. He carried her off, and they got married from another house. Everything had been got ready beforehand. There was a pursuit. But the late prince stuck up for them, and it was all settled.'

'They got married, did they? But how is it—how did you get to know?'

'We know, sir. The world's full of rumours. We know it all. It could happen to anyone. Only let me tell you, sir, in plain servants' talk, if it's come to that, you've got a rival, sir, a strong one.'

'I know, my friend, I know. So I'm relying on you. What are we to do now? What do you advise?'

'Well sir, if roughly speaking that's the style of thing you're going in for, there are things you'll

have to get, sheets, pillows, another feather-bed
—a double one, a good blanket . . . There's a
woman underneath here, sir, a common woman,
she's got a fine fox cloak. You might have a look
at that, and buy it. You could pop down and see
it now. It's just what you need now, sir, a fine
fox cloak lined with satin . . .'

'All right my friend, I agree. I rely on you
entirely. Let's have that then. But be quick
about it. For God's sake be quick! It'll soon be
eight. For God's sake be quick!'

Dropping the linen, pillows, blankets and various
oddments he had been about to bundle up,
Petrushka rushed headlong from the room. Mr.
Golyadkin dragged out the letter again, but was
unable to read it. Clutching his poor head in his
hands, he leant against the wall, dazed and incapable of thought or action. He didn't know
what was happening to him. At last, seeing the
time getting on, and still no sign of Petrushka or
the cloak, he decided to go himself. Opening
the door into the hall, he heard a hubbub and
clamour of voices down below. A number of
women living in the same block were jabbering,
shouting and arguing. He knew exactly what
about. Petrushka's voice could be heard for a
moment, then there was the sound of footsteps.

'Good God! They're bringing the whole world
into it!' groaned Mr. Golyadkin, wringing his
hands in despair. Diving back into his room, he

fell almost senseless onto the ottoman, face down-
wards on the cushion. After lying there for about
a minute, he leapt to his feet, and deciding not to
wait for Petrushka, put on his hat, overcoat and
galoshes, snatched up his note-case and charged
blindly down the stairs.

'Don't bother! It doesn't matter. I'll see to
it all myself. I shan't need you for the time being,
and everything will probably be settled for the
best meanwhile,' muttered Mr. Golyadkin, meeting Petrushka on the stairs. Then he dashed out
into the courtyard, and away. He felt sick at
heart, and was still unable to make up his
mind what to do, and how to act at this critical
juncture.

'What in heaven's name am I to do, that's the
question,' he cried in despair, as he hobbled
blindly and aimlessly along the street. 'Why did
all this have to happen? But for *this,* everything
would have been settled. One stroke, one deft,
resolute, vigorous stroke, would have put the
whole thing right at once. I'd give a finger to
do that. I even know how it could be done—
like this. "Such and such," I'd say, "it's neither
here nor there, sir, if you'll allow me to say so.
Things aren't done that way—no, sir. Impersonation won't get you anywhere here. An impostor,
sir, is good for nothing, and no use to his country.
Do you understand, sir?" That's how it would
be. But no. That's not how it is, not at all. I'm

talking through my hat like a fool—my own executioner, that's what I am. You're your own executioner! But you can see how it's happening now, you depraved man! Still, where am I to go, what am I going to do with myself now? What am I fit for? Just what, for instance, poor unworthy fellow that I am!

'Well, what now? We must get a carriage. "Have a carriage here," she says, "we'll get our little feet wet if you don't . . ." And who would have thought it? Well well, my virtuous young miss, who everyone thinks the world of, you've surpassed yourself and no mistake. And it all comes of an immoral upbringing. Now I've gone into it a bit and got the hang of it, I can see it's nothing more nor less than that. Instead of taking the stick to her now and then when she was young, they stuffed her with sweets and confectionery, and the old man slobbered all over her with his "You're my daddy's this and that, and we'll marry you to a count!" And this is what they get for it. She's shown us her hand now. "This is what we're up to," she says. Instead of keeping her at home, they send her to a boarding-school—to some French emigrée, Madame Falbala, or something of the sort. And a lot of good she's learnt there! Now she turns out like this. "Come and be happy," she says! "Be outside the windows at such and such a time in a carriage," she says, "and sing a tender Spanish ballad. I'll be waiting. I know you love me, and we'll fly together and live in a cottage." But it won't work, young lady. If that's what it's come to, it won't work, because it's against the law to take an honest, innocent young lady from her parents' house without their consent. Why do it? What need is there? She should marry who she's supposed to, as fate intended, and that's that. I'm in the service. I could lose my job through it. I might finish up in court, young lady! So that's how it is, if you didn't know. It's the work of that German woman. It all goes back to her, the witch. She's the one who started all the rumpus. Slandering a man, making up some old wives' gossip and a cock-and-bull story about him on the advice of Andrey Filippovich. It all goes back to her. How would Petrushka have got into it otherwise? What's he want here? Is it any of that scoundrel's business? No, young lady, I can't. I can't possibly. This once you must excuse me somehow. You're the source of the whole thing, young lady, not the German, not the old witch, it doesn't come from her at all, but simply and solely from you. She's a good woman, she's not to blame for anything, but you are, young lady. You're getting me accused of something I'm not guilty of . . . Look, here's a man losing control of himself, losing sight of himself, on the point of vanishing for ever—and you're talking about a wedding! And what

will be the end of it all? And how will it turn
out? I'd give a lot to know.'

Thus reasoned our hero in his despair. Returning suddenly to his immediate surroundings,
he noticed that he was standing somewhere in
Liteynaya Street. The weather was terrible. A
thaw had set in, and it was snowing and raining
just as it had been at that dreadful and never-to-
be-forgotten midnight hour when all his misfortunes had begun.

'How can you go a journey in this?' he thought.
'It's certain death. Oh God! Where am I to
find a cab here, for instance? There seems to be
some dark object on the corner there. Let's go
and investigate. Oh God!' continued our hero
as he tottered feebly in the direction of what
looked like a cab. 'No. This is what I'll do. I'll
go and throw myself at his feet, if I can, and make
humble entreaties. "Such and such," I'll say, "I
put my fate into your hands, into the hands of
my superiors. Protect me, your Excellency, show
me your support. This and that and such and such
a thing is an unlawful act," I'll say. "Don't ruin
me. I look upon you as a father. Don't forsake
me. Rescue my dignity, name and honour . . .
Deliver me from a depraved villain. He's one
man, your Excellency, and I am another. He
goes his way, and I go mine. I do, your Excellency, indeed I do. I can't resemble him," I'll
say. "Replace him, your Excellency. Order

him to be replaced, I beg you, and put an end to an ungodly and unwarranted impersonation, that it may not serve as a precedent for others. I look upon you as a father." A benevolent superior having the welfare of his subordinates at heart must surely encourage such action. There's a touch of chivalry about it. "You, my benevolent superior, I regard as a father," I'll say. "I put my fate in your hands. I'll make no objections. I trust in you. I myself withdraw from the affair." That's it!'

'Are you a cabman?'

'I am.'

'I want a cab for the evening.'

'Going far, sir?'

'For the evening, I want it, and to go wherever may be necessary.'

'You don't mean out of town?'

'Maybe, my friend. I don't know myself yet, and can't tell you. The point is, it may all turn out for the best, you see. You know how it is.'

'Yes, of course, sir. God grant as much to everyone.'

'Yes, my friend. Yes. Thank you. Well, how much will it be?'

'Do you want to go now?'

'Yes, that is—no. You'll have to wait a little at a certain spot . . . Just a little, not long . . .'

'Well, if you hire me for the whole time, I

couldn't do it for less than six roubles in weather like this.'

'All right, all right. I'll make it worth your while, old chap. You'll take me now then, will you?'

'In you get. Excuse me, I'll just put it right a second. That's it. Now in you get. Where to?'

'Izmaylovsky Bridge, my friend.'

The driver clambered onto the box, and with some difficulty dragged his two miserably-thin horses away from the hay-trough, and roused them to move in the direction of the Izmaylovsky Bridge. But all of a sudden Mr. Golyadkin tugged the cord, stopped the cab, and implored the driver to turn and go to another street instead. The driver did so, and ten minutes later Mr. Golyadkin and his newly-acquired carriage drew up before the house in which were his Excellency's apartments. He jumped down, urged the driver to wait, and with his heart in his boots, charged up to the second floor and pulled the bell. The door opened, and he found himself in his Excellency's hall.

'Is his Excellency at home?' he inquired of the servant who had opened to him.

'What do you want?' asked the servant, looking him up and down.

'I-I'm Golyadkin, the clerk, my friend. I've come to explain, tell him.'

'Wait, you can't . . .'

'I can't wait, my friend. My business is important, and doesn't admit of any delay.'

'Who are you from? Have you brought papers?'

'No. I've come on my own account. Announce me, my friend, and say I've come to explain.'

'I can't. Orders are to receive no one. He has visitors. Come at ten in the morning.'

'Announce me. I can't wait—it's impossible. You'll answer for this . . .'

'Go on, announce him. What's the matter, saving shoe-leather or something?' said another lackey, who till then had merely been lolling on a seat in the hall.

'Shoe-leather be damned! Orders were not to receive anyone, see? Their turn is mornings.'

'Go on. Afraid your tongue will come off?'

'All right, I will. I'm not afraid of my tongue coming off, but orders were as I said.—Come in here.'

Mr. Golyadkin went into the first room. There was a clock on the table. He glanced at it. It was eight-thirty. He felt torn with anguish. He was about to turn back, but at that very moment a lanky footman stationed at the door of the next room, loudly announced Mr. Golyadkin's name.

'What a voice!' he thought, in indescribable agony. '"Such and such a thing," he ought to have said, "he has most dutifully and humbly come to explain. Will you kindly see him?" Now it's ruined. All I've done has been thrown away. Still, it doesn't matter.'

There was no time for reflection however. The lackey returned, and with a 'come on', took Mr. Golyadkin into the study.

The moment he walked in, he felt as if he had been suddenly blinded, for he could see nothing. He had, however, caught a glimpse of two or three figures.

'Ah yes, those are the visitors,' flashed through his mind.

At last he was able to make out the star upon his Excellency's frock-coat; then by a gradual process he proceeded to an awareness of the black frock-coat itself, and finally received the faculty of complete vision.

'What is it?' asked a familiar voice above his head.

'Titular Counsellor Golyadkin, your Excellency.'

'Well?'

'I've come to explain.'

'What's that?'

'Yes, it's like this. I said I've come to explain, your Excellency, sir.'

'Who are you?'

'M-M-Mister Golyadkin, your Excellency, a titular counsellor.'

'Well, what do you want?'

'I'll tell him this and that,' he thought. 'I look upon him as a father. "I'm withdrawing from the matter, and protect me from my enemies," that's what I'll say.'

'What's that?'

'Of course . . .'

'Of course what?'

Mr. Golyadkin said nothing. His chin was beginning to twitch slightly.

'Well?'

'I thought it chivalrous, your Excellency. There's chivalry about it, I thought. And I look upon my departmental head as I would a father . . . Protect me, I b-b-beg you with t-t-tears in my eyes . . . s-s-such action m-m-must b-b-be encouraged . . .'

His Excellency turned away. For some minutes our hero's eyes could distinguish nothing. There was a great weight upon his chest. His lungs were bursting. He did not know where he was. He felt ashamed. He felt sad. What happened next, he had no idea.

When he recovered, he saw that his Excellency was talking to his visitors; he seemed to be debating something with them in an abrupt and forceful manner. One of the visitors our hero recognised at once. It was Andrey Filippovich. Another he did not recognise, although his face seemed familiar. He was tall, thick-set, elderly, with very bushy side-whiskers, and a keen and expressive gaze. About his neck he wore a decoration, and in his mouth was a cigar. He smoked steadily, keeping the cigar in his mouth, and every now and then glanced towards Mr. Golyadkin and nodded meaningly. Mr. Golyadkin began to feel uneasy. Shifting his gaze, he caught sight of yet another strange visitor. In a doorway, which till then our hero had as on a previous occasion taken for a mirror, *he* appeared, the *he* who is already familiar to the reader, Mr. Golyadkin's very intimate friend and acquaintance! Golyadkin junior had until this moment been in another small room, writing something in a hurry. Now, because it had evidently become necessary to do so, he emerged carrying the papers under his arm, went up to his Excellency, and while awaiting the latter's undivided attention, succeeded very cleverly in worming his way into the general counsel and confabulation, taking up a position behind Andrey Filippovich's back, and partly hidden by the cigar-smoking stranger. Golyadkin junior was clearly acutely interested in the conversation, to which he was listening in a genteel fashion, nodding assent, shifting from one foot to the other, and smiling and glancing every other minute at his Excellency, as if imploring to be allowed to put his word in.

'Wretch!' thought Mr. Golyadkin, and involuntarily took a step forward. Just then his

Excellency turned, and came rather uncertainly towards Mr. Golyadkin.

'Well, that's all right. Off you go then. I'll look into your case, and I'll get someone to show you out.' The general glanced at the stranger with the bushy side-whiskers. The latter nodded.

Mr. Golyadkin sensed and realized quite clearly that they were taking him for something that he wasn't, and not at all as they ought.

'I must explain somehow or other,' he thought. '"Such and such a thing, your Excellency," I'll say.'

In his perplexity he looked down at the floor, and was amazed to observe large white patches on his Excellency's boots.

'Surely they haven't split?' he thought. He soon discovered they had not, but were merely acting as powerful reflectors, a phenomenon fully explained by their being of shining patent leather.

'Those are what they call "high-lights",' he thought. 'That's the name that's reserved for them, especially in artists' studios. Elsewhere they're known as "bright spots".'

At this point he looked up, and saw it was time to speak, as things might easily take a turn for the worse and end badly. He took a step forward.

'"Such and such a thing," I said, your Excellency, "but impersonation will get you nowhere."'

The general made no answer, but tugged hard at the bell-pull. Our hero took another step forward.

'He's vile and perverted, your Excellency,' he said, highly agitated and sick with fear, but still pointing boldly and resolutely at his unworthy twin, who was at that moment fidgeting about near his Excellency. 'That's what I say, and I'm alluding to someone we all know.'

These words were followed by general commotion. Andrey Filippovich and the stranger nodded their heads. His Excellency, in his impatience, tugged the bell-pull with all his might to summon servants. At this juncture Golyadkin junior stepped forward.

'Your Excellency,' he said, 'I crave your permission to speak.' There was a decisive ring in his voice. Everything about him showed that he felt completely within his rights.

'May I ask,' he began, anticipating his Excellency's reply in his eagerness, and now addressing Mr. Golyadkin, 'may I ask if you know in whose presence you are thus expressing yourself, before whom you are standing, and in whose study you are?'

Golyadkin junior was unusually agitated, his face was completely red, and he was burning with anger and indignation. There were even tears in his eyes.

'The Bassavryukovs!' roared a footman at the top of his voice, appearing suddenly at the door.

'A fine noble name—they're from the Ukraine,' thought Mr. Golyadkin, and immediately felt a friendly hand rest upon his back. This was followed by another. He saw clearly that he was being steered towards the study door, while his vile twin fussed about in front, showing the way.

'It's just as it was at Olsufy Ivanovich's,' he thought, and found himself in the hall. Looking round he saw two of his Excellency's footmen and his twin.

'My friend's coat! My friend's coat! My best friend's coat!' babbled the perverted man, snatching the overcoat from one of the servants, and throwing it right over Mr. Golyadkin's head to put him to ridicule in a most blackguardly and outrageous manner. As he fought his way out from under the coat, Mr. Golyadkin could clearly hear the two footmen laughing. But paying no heed to the sounds around him, he marched out of the hall and found himself on a lighted stairway. Golyadkin junior followed.

'Good-bye, your Excellency,' he shouted after Golyadkin senior.

'Villain!' said our hero, beside himself.

'I don't mind . . .'

'Pervert!'

'Just as you like . . .' answered the worthy Golyadkin's unworthy foe from the top of the stairs, looking the former unblinkingly straight in the eye, in that peculiarly vile way of his, begging him to go on, as it were. Our hero made an indignant gesture, and ran down and out into the street. Such was his state of despair that he had no recollection at all of how or by whose agency he got into the carriage. On regaining his senses, he found that he was being driven along the Fontanka.

'We must be going to the Izmaylovsky Bridge,' he thought. There was something else he was trying to think of, but could not. It was so terrible as to defy explanation.

'Well, it doesn't matter,' he concluded, and proceeded to the Izmaylovsky Bridge.

## 13

THE weather, it seemed, was trying to change for the better. The wet snow which till then had been falling in prodigious quantities, began gradually to ease, and finally stopped altogether. The sky appeared, and here and there a tiny star began to twinkle. But it was wet and muddy underfoot, and it was muggy; Mr. Golyadkin, who had difficulty in catching his breath as it was, found it particularly so. His overcoat, which had become sodden and heavy, made him feel disagreeably warm and wet all over, while his enfeebled legs buckled beneath its weight. Sharp feverish shivers ran through his whole body. He broke into a cold sickly sweat from sheer exhaustion. Appropriate as the moment was, he quite forgot to reiterate with his customary resolution and determination his favourite phrase that it would all perhaps, somehow, in all probability, certainly turn out for the best.

'Still, none of this matters for the time being,' said our sturdy hero, still undismayed, wiping from his face the cold drops of water which were trickling from all round the brim of his saturated hat. Adding that that didn't matter either, he tried sitting down for a while on a fair-sized log

lying near a stack of firewood in Olsufy Ivanovich's courtyard. Spanish serenades and silken
ladders were, of course, past thinking about.
What he must try to think of, was some quiet
little corner which, if not altogether warm, would
at least be convenient and concealed. He was, it
may be observed in passing, strongly tempted by
that particular corner on Olsufy Ivanovich's landing where, on an earlier occasion, almost at the
beginning of this true story, he had spent over
two hours of his time standing between a cupboard and some old screens amidst all sorts ot
lumber and rubbish. He had now stood waiting
two hours in Olsufy Ivanovich's courtyard. As
far as his former quiet and convenient little spot
was concerned, there were certain disadvantages
that had not existed before. Firstly, it had probably been marked since the to-do at Olsufy
Ivanovich's last ball, and safety precautions had
probably been taken; and secondly, he had to
await the agreed signal from Klara Olsufyevna,
for there was bound to be something of the sort.
There always was, and as he said, 'We aren't the
first, and we won't be the last.' He immediately
remembered quite opportunely and by the way a
novel he had read long ago, in which the heroine
had given an agreed signal to her Alfred under
exactly similar circumstances by tying up a pink
ribbon at her window. But now, after dark,
with a St. Petersburg climate notorious for its

wetness and unreliability, a pink ribbon was out of the question; to put it briefly, it was impossible.

'No. This is no time for silken ladders,' thought our hero. 'I'd better stay quietly where I am, out of sight. That's what I'd better do.' And he selected a position facing the windows, and near the wood-stack. There were, of course, postilions and coachmen, and a number of other people walking about the courtyard, added to which there was the rattle of wheels, the snorting of horses and so forth. But for all that it was a convenient position, whether anyone saw him or not, having at least the advantage of being to some extent in shadow, so that he could observe positively everything without being himself observed. The windows were all lit up. Some sort of gala reunion was taking place at Olsufy Ivanovich's, but no music could be heard as yet.

'So it's not a ball. They're gathered for some other occasion,' thought our hero with a sinking heart. 'But was it today?' flashed through his mind. 'Maybe there's a mistake in the date. Anything is possible. Or perhaps the letter was written yesterday, and didn't reach me because that scoundrel Petrushka got mixed up in the business. Or perhaps it said tomorrow. Perhaps that's when I'm supposed to do everything and be waiting with the carriage.'

With a sudden thrill of horror, he felt in his

pocket for the letter to check the point. But to his amazement the letter was not there.

'How's this?' whispered Mr. Golyadkin, feeling more dead than alive. 'Where've I left it? Have I lost it? That's all I needed!' he concluded with a groan. 'What if it gets into the wrong hands? Perhaps it has already! Oh God! What will come of this? What will happen if . . . Oh, what hideous luck!'

He began trembling like a leaf, as it occurred to him that his shameful twin might have thrown the overcoat over him for the express purpose or purloining the letter, having got wind of it from his enemies.

'And what's more, he's seized it as evidence!' thought Mr. Golyadkin. 'But why?'

After the first numbing blow of horror, the blood rushed back to his head. Groaning, gnash-ing his teeth and clutching his heated brow, he sank down on the log, and tried to think. But his thoughts would not connect themselves to any-thing. Faces, and various long-forgotten events flashed through his mind, some vague, some vivid; silly song-tunes crept into his head. His anguish was such as it had never been before.

'Oh God,' he thought, recovering a little and suppressing his dull sobs, 'oh God, grant me firmness of spirit in the unfathomable depths of my misfortune! That I am ruined, that I have ceased to exist, there is no longer any doubt at all. And

this is in the nature of things, for it could not be
otherwise. In the first place, I've lost my job—
I've certainly done that. It was inevitable.

'Now let's suppose it all comes right somehow.
We'll assume I've got enough money to begin
with. I'll need a new place to live, and some sort
of furniture. I won't have Petrushka for a start.
I can manage without the scoundrel—get help
from the people in the house. Splendid! I can
come and go when I like, and there won't be any
Petrushka to grumble because I'm late. That's a
good way of doing it. Well, let's suppose it is,
but how is it I'm talking about completely the
wrong thing?'

His predicament again dawned upon him. He
looked around.

'Oh God! What on earth have I just been
talking about?' he wondered, clutching his burning head in utter bewilderment.

'You'll be going soon, won't you, sir?' said a
voice above him. He shuddered. Standing before
him, also wet through and chilled to the bone,
was the driver, who, growing impatient at having
nothing to do, had conceived the idea of coming
to take a look at Mr. Golyadkin behind the
firewood.

'I'm all right, my friend. I won't be long. You
wait . . .'

The driver went away, muttering to himself.

'What's he grumbling about?' thought Mr.

Golyadkin tearfully. 'I hired him for the evening, didn't I? I'm within my rights! I've taken him for the evening, and that's all there is to it. He can stand there the whole time—it's all the same. It's as I please. I go if I want to—if I don't, I don't. My standing here behind the firewood doesn't matter at all, and no one dare say anything to the contrary. If a gentleman wants to stand behind the firewood, he stands behind the firewood. He's not spoiling anyone's reputation doing that. So there it is, young lady, if you really want to know. As to living in a cottage, as you say, no one does nowadays, no one. And in our industrial age, young lady, you won't get anywhere without good behaviour. You're a dreadful example of that. "Work as a chief clerk, and live in a cottage by the sea," you say. In the first place, young lady, there are no chief clerks by the sea; and in the second, the post of chief clerk is something you and I won't get. Suppose, for the sake of example, I put in a petition, and go along and say this and that, "make me chief clerk and protect me from my enemies". "We've plenty of chief clerks," they'll tell you. "You're not at Madame Falbala's learning good behaviour now," they'll say, "and a pretty poor example you give of that." Good behaviour means staying at home, honouring your father, and not thinking of suitors before you should, young lady. There'll be suitors at the proper time. You must, or

course, exhibit talent in various ways, by playing the piano a bit sometimes, speaking French,
and knowing your history, geography, scripture
and arithmetic, but nothing more. And then
there's cooking. Cooking must be included in
every nicely-behaved girl's store of knowledge.
But what's the position? To begin with, my fine
young lady, they won't let you go. They'll
pursue you, then they'll play their trump card,
and into a nunnery with you. Then what, young
lady? What will you have me do then? Come to
a nearby hill as they do in certain silly novels,
and pine away in tears, watching the cold walls
that shut you in, and finally die as habitually
described by some horrid German poets and
novelists? Is that it? Firstly, let me tell you in
a friendly way, things aren't done like that; and
secondly, you ought to have been given a sound
beating, and your parents as well, for giving you
French books to read. You learn no good from
them. They're poison, deadly poison, young
lady! Or do you think we'll get away with it,
may I ask, and find a cottage by the sea, and bill
and coo, and discuss our various feelings, and live
happily ever afterwards? And then when there's
a little one, shall we go to our father, the Civil
Counsellor, and say, "Look, Olsufy Ivanovich,
there's a little one. Will you take this as a suitable
occasion to remove your curse and bless us both?"
No, young lady, it's not done like that. And the

main thing is there won't be any billing and cooing, so don't hope for it. Nowadays, young lady, the husband is master, and a good well-brought-up wife must humour him in every way. Tender words aren't popular any more, in our industrial age. Jean-Jacques Rousseau's times are past. Nowadays the husband comes home from the office hungry, and says, "Can't I have a little something before dinner, darling, just a mouthful of herring and a nip of vodka?" And you must have it ready, young lady. Your husband will tuck in with relish, and won't so much as give you a glance. "Run into the kitchen, poppet, and keep an eye on the dinner," he'll say. And just once a week perhaps, he'll give you a kiss, and a cold peck at that. That's what it will be like, young lady—just a cold peck. And what have I got to do with it? Why have you got me mixed up in your fancies? "To the beneficent one who suffers for my sake, and is in every way dear to my heart, etc.," that's what you said. To start with, I'm no good for you, young lady. I'm no adept at compliments, as you know yourself. I'm not fond of talking sweet-scented nonsense for the ladies. I don't like gay deceivers, and I must confess, I've never got anywhere on my looks. You'll find no bounce or false shame about me, and I tell you that now in all sincerity. An open forthright nature and common sense are the two things I possess. I have nothing

to do with intrigues. I'm no intriguer, and proud
of it. I don't go about in front of good people
wearing a mask, and to say all there is to be
said . . .'

He gave a sudden start. The dripping-wet red
beard of the cabman was again peeping over the
firewood at him.

'I'm coming now, my friend. I'm coming
directly, you know,' he quavered feebly.

The cabman scratched the back of his head,
ran his hand over his beard, stepped back a pace,
stopped, and looked at him mistrustfully.

'I'm coming now, my friend. I must just wait
a teeny second, you see.'

'Don't you want to drive anywhere at all?'
asked the cabman, making a direct and determined approach.

'Yes, I'm coming. I'm waiting, you see.'

'I see.'

'You see, I . . . What village are you from,
my friend?'

'I'm a serf.'

'Got a good master?'

'Not bad.'

'Stay here for a bit, my friend. Have you been
in St. Petersburg long?'

'A year I've been driving.'

'And are you all right?'

'Not bad.'

'Well, you should thank Providence, my friend.

You look for a good man. They're rare nowadays. A good man will see to your comfort,
will give you meat and drink. But sometimes,
my friend, you see even rich men weeping . . .
You see a pitiful example—that's how it is, my
dear fellow . . .'

The cabman suddenly seemed to feel sorry for
him.

'I'll hang on, sir. Will you be waiting long?'

'No, my dear chap, I—er—you know what it
is . . . I won't wait any more. What do you
think? I rely on you. I won't wait any more.'

'Don't you want to drive anywhere?'

'No, my friend, no. But I'll make it worth
your while. What's the damage, my dear fellow?'

'What we agreed, sir. I've had a long wait,
and you wouldn't do a chap down, sir.'

'Well, here you are then.' He gave the cabman
the full six roubles, and having seriously made
up his mind to waste no more time, but to clear
off before something unpleasant happened—particularly, as with the matter settled and the
cabman dismissed, there was nothing else to wait
for—he walked out of the courtyard, turned left
through the gate, and breathless but rejoicing,
set off as fast as his legs would carry him.

'It may all turn out for the best,' he thought.
'And this way I've avoided trouble.' His mind
suddenly felt unusually at ease.

'If it only would turn out for the best!' he thought, but did not believe that it would.

'I know what . . . No. I'd better try a different approach. Or wouldn't it be better for me to . . .'

While searching to relieve the doubts that were thus assailing him, he ran as far as the Semyonovsky Bridge, where he cautiously decided to go back.

'That's the best thing,' he thought. 'I'd better try a different approach. This is what I'll do—I'll just be an outside observer, and nothing more. "I'm an onlooker, an outsider, that's all," I'll say. And whatever happens it won't be me who's to blame. That's it. That's how it will be now.'

Our hero did indeed do as he had decided and went back, and went all the more readily for having, thanks to a happy thought, become an outsider.

'It's the best thing. You're not answerable for anything, and you'll see what you should.'

His calculations were perfectly correct, and there was nothing more to it. Reassured, he stole back into the peaceful and soothingly protective shadow of the wood-stack. This time he did not have to watch and wait for long. All of a sudden there was a strange commotion at every window; figures appeared and disappeared; the curtains were drawn back, and Olsufy Ivanovich's windows were crammed with people peering out and looking for something in the courtyard. Our hero followed the general commotion with

interest and curiosity from the security of his
wood-stack, craning his head just as far out to
left and right as the short shadow afforded by
his cover would allow. Suddenly he was filled
with panic, he shuddered, he almost collapsed with
the horror of it. He realized at once. They were
not just looking for anything or anybody, but
for *him*. They were all gazing and pointing in
his direction. Escape was impossible—they'd see!
Panic-stricken, he pressed himself to the wood-
stack as tightly as he could. Only then did he
observe that the treacherous shadow had played
him false by failing to cover him completely.
Had it only been possible, he would at that
moment with the greatest pleasure in the world
have crawled into any mouse-hole the wood-
stack might offer, and sat quiet. But it was out
of the question. In his agony he stared at all the
windows at once, boldly and openly. It was the
best thing to do. Suddenly he blushed with
fiery shame. They had all seen him at the same
time. They were all beckoning, nodding, calling.
Several of the windows clicked open. Several
voices began shouting something at him simultaneously.

'I'm surprised they don't whip these wretched
girls when they're children,' he muttered, completely disconcerted.

All of a sudden, tripping, whirling and pranc-
ing down the steps, breathless, hatless and wearing

just his uniform, came *he*—someone we know—
with an air that treacherously expressed how most
frightfully glad he was to see Mr. Golyadkin.

'You here, Yakov Petrovich?' warbled the
notoriously worthless man. 'You'll catch a cold.
It's chilly. Come along in.'

'No. I'm all right, Yakov Petrovich,' mumbled
our hero submissively.

'You *must*, Yakov Petrovich. They most
humbly beg you—they're waiting for us. "Do
us the pleasure of bringing in Yakov Petrovich,"
they said.'

'No, Yakov Petrovich, you see, I'd better . . .
I'd better be off home,' said our hero, so horrified
and abashed that he felt he was being frozen to
death and roasted alive at the same time.

'Not at all, not at all!' twittered the odious
man. 'Nothing of the sort! Come on!' he said
firmly, dragging Golyadkin senior towards the
steps. The latter did not want to go in the least,
but went, because to kick and struggle with
everyone watching would have been stupid. To
say that he went is not, however, strictly accurate,
for he had little idea what was happening to
him.

Before he had time to tidy himself or recover
his senses, he was in the reception-room. Pale,
ruffled and dishevelled, he gazed dully around,
and saw a multitude of people. It was horrible!
The reception-room and everywhere else was

filled to overflowing. There were people without number, there were galaxies of lovely ladies, and they were all milling and pressing around him, and bearing him, as he clearly perceived, in a definite direction.

'This isn't the way to the door,' flashed through his mind, and indeed it was not. He was heading straight for the comfortable arm-chair of Olsufy Ivanovich. On one side of this, pale, languid and melancholy, but sumptuously arrayed, stood Klara Olsufyevna. Mr. Golyadkin was particularly struck by the wonderfully effective tiny white flowers adorning her raven hair. On the other side, in a black morning coat, and wearing his new decoration in his buttonhole, stood Vladimir Semyonovich. Mr. Golyadkin was, as we have already intimated, being conducted straight towards Olsufy Ivanovich; steering him by one arm was Golyadkin junior, who had now assumed an extraordinarily decorous and well-intentioned air—which was a source of some gratification to our hero—and at the other, looking very grave, was Andrey Filippovich.

'What's this?' wondered Mr. Golyadkin.

The moment he saw before whom he was being taken, his brain cleared with lightning rapidity. He thought in a flash of the purloined letter . . . With a feeling of immeasurable anguish, he stood before Olsufy Ivanovich's chair.

'What am I to do now?' he thought. 'Be

bold, speak out, of course—but with a certain nobleness of manner. This and that, I'll say, and so on.'

But what our hero had apparently been fearing, did not happen. Olsufy Ivanovich seemed to receive him quite well, and although he did not proffer his hand, he did at least gaze at him, and shake his awe-inspiring grey head in a sad, solemn, but at the same time affable manner. So at least it seemed to Mr. Golyadkin. In those lustreless eyes he seemed even to detect a glistening tear. Looking up, he saw what appeared to be a tiny tear sparkling upon the lashes of Klara Olsufyevna. Vladimir Semyonovich seemed also to have something of the sort in his eyes. No less eloquent of sympathy than the general lachrymation, was the calm, inviolable dignity of Andrey Filippovich; while the young man who at one time had looked very much the important counsellor was at this moment sobbing bitterly. Or perhaps it all merely seemed so to Mr. Golyadkin because he was himself overcome with powerful emotion, and could distinctly feel the hot tears coursing down his frozen cheeks. Reconciled with man and destiny, filled at that moment with affection not only for Olsufy Ivanovich, but for all the guests put together—even for his pernicious twin, who was now apparently not pernicious at all and not even his twin, but a stranger and a perfectly amiable person in his own right—Mr. Golyadkin was about

to pour forth his soul to Olsufy Ivanovich in a
moving speech, his voice choked with sobs. But
his feelings were too much for him. His voice
failed him, and he could only point eloquently
at his heart. At last, wishing no doubt to spare
the grey-haired old man, Andrey Filippovich
drew Mr. Golyadkin a little to one side, and left
him, completely at liberty it seemed. Smiling,
muttering to himself, a little perplexed but at all
events almost reconciled with man and destiny,
our hero began to move through the dense throng
of guests. Everyone made way and regarded him
with strange curiosity, and a concern that was
puzzling and unaccountable. Our hero passed
into the next room, and received the same attention. He was dimly aware of the whole crowd
following him, watching his every step, dis-
coursing quietly on something of extreme interest,
shaking their heads, debating and whispering.
He would have liked to know what it was all
about. Looking round, he noticed Golyadkin
junior beside him. Feeling obliged to catch hold
of his arm and take him aside, Mr. Golyadkin
earnestly begged him to support him in all future
undertakings, and not to abandon him at a critical
moment. Golyadkin junior nodded gravely,
and gave him a firm squeeze of the hand.
So overwhelming was our hero's emotion, that
his heart trembled within him. But then he
gasped for breath. He felt a terrible weight upon

his chest. He felt oppressed and stifled beneath
the stare of so many eyes ... He caught a glimpse
of the counsellor wearing a wig. He was eyeing
him in a stern, searching manner, that showed he
had been quite unmollified by the general aura
of sympathy. Our hero was on the point of
marching over to him, giving him a smile, and
clearing things up immediately, but somehow
did not manage to do this. For a moment he
almost lost consciousness; memory and senses
forsook him. When he came to, he noticed that
the guests had formed a large circle around him.
His name was suddenly shouted from the next
room, and the shout was immediately taken up
by the whole crowd. Uproar and excitement
ensued. Everyone rushed for the door, almost
carrying him along with them. Close beside
him was the stony-hearted counsellor in the wig.
The latter finally took him by the arm, and sat
him on a chair next to his, directly opposite but
some distance away from where Olsufy Ivanovich
was sitting. Everyone else in the place sat down
on several rows of chairs arranged around Mr.
Golyadkin and Olsufy Ivanovich. All grew
hushed and still. Everyone was observing a
solemn silence and gazing towards Olsufy Ivanovich, obviously expecting something rather out
of the ordinary. Mr. Golyadkin noticed the other
Mr. Golyadkin and Andrey Filippovich sitting
next to Olsufy Ivanovich, and facing the coun-

sellor. The silence lasted a long time. They were, in fact, waiting for something.

'Just as it is in any family when someone's going on a long journey,' thought our hero. 'It only wants us to get up, and say a prayer.'

All Mr. Golyadkin's reflections were interrupted by a sudden strange commotion. The long-expected was happening.

'He's coming! He's coming!' ran through the crowd.

'Who's coming?' ran through Mr. Golyadkin's head. A peculiar sensation caused him to shudder.

'Now!' said the counsellor, looking intently at Andrey Filippovich. The latter shot a glance at Olsufy Ivanovich, who nodded gravely and solemnly.

'Up we get,' said the counsellor, hoisting Mr. Golyadkin to his feet. Everyone rose. The counsellor then took Golyadkin senior by the arm, Andrey Filippovich did the same to Golyadkin junior, and surrounded by the eagerly expectant crowd, they solemnly brought these two completely identical beings together. Our hero, perplexed, began to look about him, but was immediately checked, and shown Golyadkin junior, who was offering him his hand.

'They want to reconcile us,' thought our hero suddenly, and greatly touched, he held out his hand to Golyadkin junior, then offered his cheek. The other did likewise. At this juncture Golyadkin

senior thought he saw his treacherous friend
smile, and give a quick mischievous wink to all
around; he thought he detected something sinister
in his face, and thought he even grimaced as he
gave his Judas kiss. His head rang. Darkness
swam before his eyes. A whole procession of
identical Golyadkins seemed to be bursting loudly
in at every door. But it was too late. The re-
sounding treacherous kiss had been given.

At this point something quite unexpected
occurred. The door flew open with a bang, and
on the threshold stood a man whose very appearance made Mr. Golyadkin's blood run cold. He
stood rooted to the spot. His cry died away
unuttered. His chest felt constricted. But he had
known it all beforehand, and had long anticipated
something of the sort. Gravely and solemnly,
the stranger advanced towards him. It was a
figure he knew very well, and had seen often,
very often—that same day even. It was a thick-
set man in a black morning coat; about his neck
he wore the cross of an important decoration;
he had very black bushy side-whiskers; all that
was missing was the cigar. His eyes froze Mr.
Golyadkin with horror. With a grave, solemn
visage, this terrible man approached the sorry
hero of our tale. Our hero stretched out his
hand. The stranger took it, and pulled him along
after him . . . Our hero gazed around, crushed
and bewildered.

'It's Krestyan Ivanovich Rutenspitz, doctor of medicine and surgery, an old friend of yours, Yakov Petrovich,' twittered a repulsive voice right in Mr. Golyadkin's ear. He glanced round. It was his abominable blackguardly twin. His face was shining with an unseemly glee that boded ill. He was rubbing his hands in ecstasy, rapturously rolling his head, and fussing delightedly around all and sundry. He looked ready to dance with joy on the spot. Finally he leapt forward, and seizing a candle from one of the servants, lighted the way for Dr. Rutenspitz and Mr. Golyadkin. The latter clearly heard everyone in the room rushing after them, crowding and squashing each other, and all repeating with one accord: 'It's all right. Don't be afraid, Yakov Petrovich. It's an old friend and acquaintance of yours—Dr. Rutenspitz.'

They came at last to the brightly-illuminated main staircase, and this too was crowded with people. The front door was thrown open with a crash, and Mr. Golyadkin found himself on the steps with Dr. Rutenspitz. Drawn up at the bottom was a carriage and four. The horses were snorting impatiently. Three bounds, and the maliciously gloating Golyadkin junior was down the steps and opening the carriage-door. Dr. Rutenspitz motioned Mr. Golyadkin to get in. There was no need for that at all, however, for there were quite enough people to help him up.

Sick with horror, he looked back. The whole of the brightly-lit staircase was thick with people. Inquisitive eyes were watching him from all sides. On the topmost landing in his comfortable arm-chair, presided Olsufy Ivanovich, watching with attentive interest all that was taking place below. They were all waiting. A murmur of impatience ran through the crowd as Mr. Golyadkin looked back.

'I trust there is nothing reprehensible . . . concerning my official relationships . . . that could provoke any severe measure . . . and excite public attention,' said our hero in his confusion. There was general hubbub. Everyone shook their heads. Tears gushed from Mr. Golyadkin's eyes.

'In that case I am ready . . . I have complete faith in Dr. Rutenspitz, and give my fate into his hands . . .'

No sooner had he said this, than there burst from those around a shout of joy, ear-splitting and terrible, that was echoed ominously by the whole waiting throng. Then Dr. Rutenspitz and Andrey Filippovich each took one of Mr. Golyadkin's arms and started putting him into the carriage—the double, in his usual blackguardly way, assisting from behind. The unhappy Golyadkin senior took one last look at everything and everybody, and trembling like a drenched kitten —if one may use the simile—he climbed into the carriage. Dr. Rutenspitz got in immediately after. The door slammed. The whip cracked. And the horses drew the carriage away . . . Everyone dashed in pursuit. The shrill, frantic cries of all his enemies rang after him like so many farewells. For a while he caught glimpses of people around the carriage as it bore him away, but gradually they were left behind, and finally they were lost to sight completely. Mr. Golyadkin's unseemly twin stayed longer than all the rest. Hands thrust into the pockets of his green uniform trousers and with a satisfied look on his face, he kept pace with the carriage, jumping up first on one side, then on the other, and sometimes, seizing and hanging from the window frame, he would pop his head in and blow farewell kisses at Mr. Golyadkin. But he, too, began at last to tire. His appearances became fewer and fewer, and finally he vanished for good. Mr. Golyadkin's heart ached dully within him. Fiery blood was rushing to his head. He was suffocating. He wanted to unbutton coat and shirt, bare his breast, and fling snow and cold water upon it. At last he fell unconscious . . .

When he came to, he saw the horses were taking him along a road he did not know. Dark forest loomed to left and right. It was lonely and desolate. Suddenly he grew stark with horror. Two burning eyes were staring out of the darkness at him, two eyes burning with evil and infernal glee. This wasn't Dr. Rutenspitz! Who was it? Or was it him? It was! Not the earlier Dr. Rutenspitz, but another, a terrible Dr. Rutenspitz!

'I-I'm all right, I think, Dr. Rutenspitz,' began our hero, timid and trembling, and wishing to propitiate the terrible Dr. Rutenspitz by a show of meekness and obedience.

'You vill haf lodging, viz firevood light and service, vich is more zan you deserf,' came Dr. Rutenspitz' reply, stern and dreadful as a judge's sentence.

Our hero gave a scream, and clutched his head. Alas! He had felt this coming for a long time!